Edward Stratemeyer

The Young Auctioneer

The polishing of a rolling stone

Edward Stratemeyer

The Young Auctioneer
The polishing of a rolling stone

ISBN/EAN: 9783337288549

Printed in Europe, USA, Canada, Australia, Japan

Cover: Foto ©Andreas Hilbeck / pixelio.de

More available books at **www.hansebooks.com**

YOUNG AUCTIONEERS;

OR,

THE POLISHING OF A ROLLING STONE.

By EDWARD STRATEMEYER,

Author of "Bound to be an Electrician," "Shorthand Tom,"
"Fighting for his Own," etc., etc.

W. L. ALLISON COMPANY,
NEW YORK.

CONTENTS.

PREFACE.

———

"THE Young Auctioneers" forms the initial volume of a line of juvenile stories called "The Working Upward Series."

The tale is complete in itself, and tells of the adventures of a homeless, although not a penniless youth, who strikes up an acquaintanceship with another young fellow experienced as an auctioneer. The two purchase a horse and wagon, stock up with goods, and take to the road. The partners pass through a number of more or less trying experiences, and the younger lad is continually on the lookout for his father, who has broken out of an asylum while partly deranged in mind over the loss of his wife and his fortune.

I have endeavored in this tale to give a faithful picture of life among a certain class of traveling salesmen who are but little known to the world at large, especially to those who inhabit our large cities. In country places the traveling auctioneer is looked for as a matter of course, and he is treated according to the humor of the inhabitants, or rather, according to the merits or demerits of the "bargains" offered on a previous trip.

I sincerely trust that my numerous boy readers will find the tale to their liking, and that the moral —to lead an upright, honest life under any and all circumstances—will not escape them.

EDWARD STRATEMEYER.

THE YOUNG AUCTIONEER.

CHAPTER I.

MATT ATTENDS A SALE.

" Now, ladies and gentlemen, what am I offered for this elegant vase, imported direct from Italy, a most marvelous piece of workmanship, worth every cent of twenty-five dollars? Who will start it at five dollars? Start it at four? Start it at three? At two? At one dollar? What is that—fifty cents? Rather low, lady, but as I said before, these goods must be sold, regardless of the prices obtained. Fifty cents, it is! Fifty—fifty! Who will make it one dollar?"

" Sixty!"

"What, only sixty? Well, well, well! Never mind, the goods must go, and sixty cents is better than nothing. Sixty—sixty——"

" Seventy-five!"

" Eighty!"

" One dollar !"

"At last I am offered one dollar ! Think of it ! One dollar for a beautiful vase such as might well adorn the home of a Gould, or a Vanderbilt ! But such is life. One dollar—one dollar——"

" One and a quarter !"

" One and a half !"

" One and a half is offered ! Oh, what a shame, ladies and gentlemen ; a paltry dollar and a half for an article worth, at the very lowest estimate, twenty-five dollars. Who makes it two dollars ?"

" Two !"

" Two and a half !"

" Three !"

" Three and a quarter !"

" Three and a quar— Ah, four dollars ? Four dollars ! Who says five ? Going at four—at four— at four. Four and a half—four and a quarter—this is your last chance, remember. Did you say five, sir ? No ? Well, four it is, then. Going—going— the last chance, ladies and gentlemen ! Going— going—gone, to the lady in the brown dress, Andrew, for four dollars !"

The scene was a small store on Nassau street near Fulton street, in New York City. Outside of the open doorway hung a red flag, indicative of an auction sale. The single window of the place was crowded with vases, imitation marble statues, plated tableware, and gorgeous lamps of highly-polished metal.

Among these articles was a sign in black letters on white cardboard bearing these words:

ROYAL CONSIGNMENT AUCTION CO.,
Sales Daily from 10 A.M. to 3 P.M.

Inside, toward the rear, there was a small raised platform, and upon this stood the auctioneer, a tall, thin-faced man, with sharp black eyes, and rather a squeaky voice. To one side was his assistant, a much younger and much more pleasant-looking individual, who wrapped up the articles sold and collected for them.

It was between twelve and one o'clock in the day, and the auction store was crowded with business people, who, during their lunch-time, had dropped in to see what was going on, and, possibly, make a purchase. There were middle-aged business men, young clerks, and several young ladies, and all appeared interested in the mild excitement attending the disposal of the goods.

Among the young people present was a boy of fifteen, whose clothing, although not of a fashionable cut, was, nevertheless, neat and clean. He had

dark curly hair, and his face was as honest in
appearance as it was fearless and handsome.

The youth was as much interested in the sale as
though he was buying half the articles auctioned
off, although he had not enough in his trousers
pocket to even start bidding, for no bid of less than
twenty-five cents was recognized by the auctioneer
in beginning a sale.

The vase disposed of, the auctioneer's assistant
brought forth from a side shelf a piece of imitation
marble statuary, representing three doves bearing a
wreath of flowers between them. The bit of bric-
a-brac looked quite nice, but as it was but imitation
marble, it was not worth more than two dollars, if
as much.

"Now, here we have as fine a piece of Italian
marble as was ever brought to New York," began
the auctioneer, holding up the piece in question.
"And the work upon it cannot to-day be excelled
by any sculptors on this side of the Atlantic. How
beautiful are those three doves, and how natural
that wreath! Examine the piece for yourselves,
ladies and gentlemen. It is genuine Italian marble,
and will not go to pieces in your hands. There you
are, sir."

The bit of statuary was handed to a gentleman
who stood directly in front of the auctioneer. He

gave it a hasty glance and then started to hand it back.

"Pass it through the crowd, please. I want every one to be convinced of its quality before I attempt to sell it!" bawled the auctioneer, and the gentleman handed it to the man next to him.

Thus started, the bit of bric-a-brac traveled from one hand to another until it reached a heavy-set man with red mustache, who stood but a couple of yards from the doorway.

"Humph!" muttered the man, as he turned over the article in contempt. "I wouldn't give a dollar a cartload for them. Here you are!"

As he finished, he thrust the piece of bric-a-brac toward a young lady who had just entered. She drew back in surprise, not knowing what his action meant. The statuary left the man's hand, touched the young lady's arm, and then fell to the floor with a crash, and was broken into a dozen pieces.

The young lady uttered a slight shriek of surprise at the accident, and instantly the crowd looked toward her, and then at the auctioneer.

"Here, who broke that?" demanded the auctioneer, in an entirely different tone of voice, as he left his stand and hurried to the spot.

"That young lady," replied a fellow who had

not seen the movements of the man with the red mustache.

"No! no! I did not do it!" cried the young lady, shrinking back. "I did not touch the piece, sir."

"Well, but it's right at your feet, madam; you must have let it fall," said the auctioneer harshly.

"I did not, sir."

"Well, who did, then?"

"A man who ran out as soon as the statuary was broken."

"Oh, pshaw! It isn't likely a man would run away like that."

"The young lady speaks the truth, sir," put in the boy previously mentioned. "The man shoved the statue toward her, and when she drew back it slipped from his hand to the floor. She was not in the least responsible."

"Thank you for that, Matt Lincoln," said the young lady, with a grateful nod. "I shall not forget this service."

"Oh, that's all right, Miss Bartlett," returned the boy, blushing. "I like to be of service to you."

"You evidently seem to know this young lady?" said the auctioneer, turning to Matt Lincoln.

"I do; she is the stenographer at our office. That's how I came to notice her when she came in."

"No wonder you try to shield her!" sneered the auctioneer. "But I can't afford to let this matter pass. You will have to pay for the damages done, madam. The cost price of that piece of bric-a-brac was ten dollars, but I'll throw off two dollars and call it eight."

CHAPTER II.

A LIVELY DISCUSSION.

At the intimation that she must pay eight dollars, the face of the young lady stenographer grew pale, while that of Matt Lincoln flushed up.

"I—I cannot pay the money!" gasped Ida Bartlett. "I have no such amount with me."

"It's a swindle!" burst in Matt Lincoln indignantly. "Don't you pay a cent, Miss Bartlett. It was not your fault, and he cannot force you to pay."

"Shut right up!" snarled the auctioneer, turning to Matt fiercely. "Unless you want to get yourself into trouble."

"I won't shut up and see this young lady ill-treated!" retorted Matt, flushing still more. "You may think you can ride over me, but you can't do it. I'll——"

"Hush, Matt!" pleaded the stenographer, catching him by the arm. "Do not say anything rash."

"But, Miss Bartlett, this chap wants to force you into paying for something you didn't do! I wouldn't stand it! I'd fight him first!"

"You would, would you?" growled the auctioneer, his face growing dark and sour,

"Yes, I would!" retorted the boy defiantly. "I'm not afraid of you!"

"Say, that boy's game!" laughed a bystander,

"Yes, a regular little bantam," replied another.

"I'll settle with you in a minute," said the auctioneer, finding he could not silence Matt. "Now, madam, do you intend to pay for the damage done or not?"

"I did not do the damage, and I cannot see how you can ask me to pay," faltered Ida Bartlett.

"I have proof that you let the piece of bric-a-brac fall."

"The chap who says he saw her drop it had his back turned at the time," put in Matt, and turning to the individual in question, he added: "Can you swear that you saw the piece of statuary leave her hand?"

"N-no, I can't do that," returned the fellow slowly. "But it went down at her feet, and——"

"You imagined the rest," finished Matt. "I told you so," he went on triumphantly.

"See here; you shut up," cried the auctioneer, losing his temper. "Dilks, come here and help me," he went on, appealing to the assistant he had before called Andrew.

The assistant auctioneer came forward upon this. His face wore a troubled look, as if he did not relish the duty he was called upon to perform.

"I'm afraid there is some mistake here, Mr. Gulligan," he said in a low tone, meant only for the auctioneer's ears.

"Some mistake!" howled Caleb Gulligan, for such was the auctioneer's name. "I don't make mistakes."

"I saw the man run out as soon as the statuary was broken, and by his manner I am sure he must be the guilty party."

"See here, Andrew Dilks, who is running this establishment?" stormed Caleb Gulligan wrathfully. "I lay the accident at the door of the young woman, and, as the man is gone, she will pay the bill—or take the consequences."

The assistant auctioneer flushed up at these words. It was plain to see that he was an honest young man, and did not like such underhand work.

"Perhaps she hasn't the money to pay?"

"Then she must take the consequences," replied the auctioneer sourly.

"Not much!" put in Matt, who had overheard the best part of the conversation between Caleb Gulligan and his assistant. "Miss Bartlett, if I was

you I wouldn't stay here another minute," he went
on to the stenographer, in a whisper.

"Why, what would you do?" she returned.

"Skip out. They haven't any right to make you
trouble."

"But, Matt, that would not be right."

"Never mind; go ahead. You haven't any friend
here but me. Mr. Fenton wouldn't help you any,
even if you ask him."

The young lady stood still for a moment, and
then made a sudden movement for the doorway.
Caleb Gulligan rushed after her, only to find Matt
Lincoln barring his progress.

"Get out of my way, boy!"

"Which way?" queried Matt coolly.

"You rat! Out of my way!"

The auctioneer placed his hand upon the boy's
arm, with the intention of hurling him aside. But,
strange to say, although he was taller than the
youth, he could not budge the latter for several seconds, and by that time the young lady had disappeared, swallowed up in the noonday crowd which
surged past the door.

"Now see what you have done!" stormed Caleb
Gulligan wrathfully. "You have aided that young
woman to escape!"

"That's just what I meant to do," returned Matt,

with a coolness that would have been exasperating to even a less sensitive man than the crusty auctioneer.

"I shall hold you responsible for it!"

"I don't care if you do," was Matt's dogged reply. "She's my friend, and I always stick up for my friends."

At this last remark there was a low murmur of approval from those gathered about. Evidently, the boy's unpolished but honest manner had won considerable admiration.

"Do you know that I can have you locked up?"

"What for?"

"For aiding her to escape."

"Didn't she have a right to hurry away if she wanted to go? It's almost one o'clock—I'll have to be off myself soon, if I want to keep my job."

There was a laugh at this, and half a dozen looked at their watches and left.

"If you please," put in the assistant nervously. "Had we not better go on with the sales? The crowd will be gone before long. We might make more than what was lost here."

"Certainly, go on with the sales," howled Caleb Gulligan. "I will take care of this young rascal, and find out what has become of that young woman."

"And that man," began the assistant.

"Never mind the man; the young woman shall pay for the damage done, and she can fix it up with the man afterward, if she wishes. I am not going to stand the loss."

"It seems to me you are making an awful row over a fifteen-cent piece of plaster-of-paris," said Matt to Gulligan, as Andrew Dilks turned toward the auctioneer's stand. "Why didn't you ask me to pay for the stuff and done?"

"Plaster-of-paris!" cried the auctioneer wrathfully. "That is real Italian marble——"

"Made in Centre street," interrupted Matt.

"And it is worth every cent of ten dollars——"

"Ten dollars a carload, you mean," went on the boy. "Come, let go of me; I've got to go to work."

"You'll go to the Tombs!"

"No, I won't. I have done nothing wrong, and I want you to let go of me."

Matt began to struggle, much to the delight of the spectators, who refused to listen to what the assistant auctioneer might have to say from the stand.

"I'll teach you a lesson!" fumed Caleb Gulligan. "How do you like that?"

He swung Matt around and caught him by the throat and the collar. But only for an instant was he able to hold the boy in that fashion. Matt squirmed and twisted like an eel, and suddenly gave the old auctioneer a push which sent him sprawling upon his back.   Before Caleb Gulligan could recover, Matt was out of the door and running like a deer up Nassau street.

"Hi! hi! stop him!" roared the old auctioneer "He must not get away."

"Stop him yourself, then," said one of the by standers heartlessly.   "We have nothing to do with your quarrel with the boy."

"You are in league with him," fumed Caleb Gulligan, as he scrambled to his feet.   "But, never mind, I'll catch him!"

He ran out of the auction store and gazed per plexedly up and down into the crowd.   It was useless.   Matt Lincoln, like his friend, Ida Bartlett, had disappeared.

CHAPTER III.

SOMETHING OF THE PAST.

Matt Lincoln did not stop until he reached Temple Court, as that large office-building on the corner of Nassau and Beekman streets is called. Then he drew a long breath as he took a stand in one corner of a side corridor.

"There, I've put my foot into it again, I suppose," he said, somewhat dismally. "I reckon old Uncle Dan was right, I'm the rolling stone that's forever getting into a hole and out without settling anywhere. But I couldn't stand it to see Miss Bartlett threatened. It wasn't a fair thing to do, and that auctioneer ought to be run out of the city. I suppose he'll be after my scalp now."

Matt Lincoln was sixteen years of age. For the past two years he had been depending entirely upon himself, and during that time he had, indeed, been a rolling stone, although not entirely without an object.

Up to his tenth year Matt had lived with his

father and mother in the Harlem district of the great metropolis. He had attended one of the public schools, and, take it all in all, had been a happy boy.

Then came a cloud over the Lincoln home. Mr. Lincoln was interested, as a speculator, in some mines in Montana, and by a peculiar manipulation of the stocks of these mines he lost every dollar of his hard-earned savings. He was an over-sensitive man, and these losses preyed upon his mind until he was affected mentally, and had to be sent to an asylum.

For several months Mrs. Lincoln and Matt paid weekly visits to the asylum to see the father and husband, and they were beginning to rejoice over the thought that Mr. Lincoln would soon be himself once more, when one day Mrs. Lincoln fell down in the middle of Broadway, and a heavily-loaded truck passed directly over her chest.

When the poor woman was picked up it was found she was unconscious. An ambulance was at once summoned, and she was conveyed to one of the city hospitals. Here Matt visited her, and listened to her last words of love and advice. She died before sunrise the next day, and three days later was buried.

If his mother's unexpected death was a shock to

poor Matt, it was even more of a one to Mr. Lincoln. Again was the father and husband's mind unbalanced; this time far worse than ever before. He escaped from the asylum, made a dramatic appearance at the home during the burial services, and then disappeared, no one knew where.

Matt's only remaining relative at this time was his Uncle Dan, a brother to Mr. Lincoln. He took charge of Matt, and took the boy to his home in Bridgeport, Connecticut. At the same time a diligent search for Mr. Lincoln was begun.

The search for Matt's father was unsuccessful, although continued for several weeks. It was learned that he had boarded a train in Jersey City bound for Philadelphia, but there all trace of his whereabouts was lost.

Matt lived with his Uncle Dan for four years. He went to school in Bridgeport part of the time, and when not learning, could be found at Mr. Lincoln's ship chandlery, a large place, situated down near the docks.

It would seem that the tragic occurrences through which he had passed would have made Matt melancholy and low-spirited, but such was not the case. Mrs. Lincoln had naturally been of a light heart, and the boy partook of much of his mother's disposition. He loved a free-and-easy life, loved to roam

from place to place. With a captain who was a
friend of Uncle Dan, he had made a trip to Bangor
and Augusta, and he had likewise put in two weeks
at a lumber camp in Maine, and a month during
the summer at a hotel among the White Mountains,
doing odd jobs for the proprietor.

"A rolling stone and nothing less," Uncle Dan
had called him, over and over again, and the title
seemed to fit Matt exactly.

At length, when Matt was fourteen years old,
Uncle Dan Lincoln, who was then an elderly man,
was taken with pneumonia, and died two weeks
later. His wife, a crabbed woman, who detested
Matt, and was glad when he was out of the house,
at once sold out the chandlery, and went to live
with her folks in a small village in Vermont. Thus
Matt was thrown out upon his own resources with
no capital but a ten-dollar bill, which his Uncle Dan
had quietly slipped into his hand only a few days
before the end.

Matt remained around Bridgeport but two days
after his uncle's funeral. Then he struck up a bargain with the captain of a schooner which was
loaded with freight for Philadelphia, and sailed for
that city.

When no trace of Matt's father could be found
the detectives who had been put on the case de-

clared their belief that the poor man had drowned himself in the Delaware River. This belief was strengthened when some clothing that looked like that which the demented man had worn was found in a secluded spot not far from the river bank.

But Matt could not bring himself to believe that his father was dead. There was a hope in his breast which amounted almost to a conviction that some day he would again find his parent, alive and well.

Yet Matt's search in and around Philadelphia, lasting several months, was unsuccessful. His money was soon spent, and then he started to tramp from Philadelphia to his former home, New York.

This tramp, of about one hundred miles by the various turnpikes through New Jersey, took the boy just one week, and when he arrived in the metropolis, botlr his clothing and his shoes were considerably worn. But he brushed up, and lost no time in hunting up work, knowing that it would never do to remain idle.

For two days Matt was without employment. Then he thought of the man who had sold his father the mining shares, Mr. Randolph Fenton, and he paid the stock-broker a visit at his offices, on Broad street, just off of Wall street.

As it happened, Randolph Fenton was just then in need of a boy to run errands and do copying, and after a talk with Matt, he hired him at a salary of four dollars a week.

"I'll take you in because I thought so much of your dear father," explained Randolph Fenton. "We were great friends, you must know, and I feel it my duty to do something for his son."

Randolph Fenton spoke very nicely, but Matt soon found that he was by no means the kind-hearted gentleman he wished to appear. In reality, he was very mean and close. He worked his clerks almost to death, and such a thing as a raise in salary was unknown in the office.

But Matt found it would do no good to complain. Times were just then somewhat hard, and another place was not easy to obtain. He decided to make the most of it until times grew better, and in this resolve remained with Randolph Fenton week after week until the opening of this story.

Matt had been sent by Randolph Fenton on an errand to Temple Court, to be done as soon as the boy had finished lunch. Waiting for another minute to make certain that he was not being followed, the boy hurried to one of the elevators, and was lifted to the third floor.

The errand was quickly transacted, and with several books under his arm for his employer, Matt started on the return to the offices in Broad street.

Not wishing to be seen in the vicinity of the auction store, Matt turned down Park Row instead of Nassau street, and so continued down Broadway, his intention being to pass through Wall to Broad.

He had just reached the corner of Fulton street when some one tapped him upon the shoulder, and turning, he found himself confronted by Andrew Dilks, the old auctioneer's assistant.

CHAPTER IV.

AN INTERESTING PROPOSITION.

On catching sight of Andrew Dilks Matt's first thought was to break and run. But a second look into the old auctioneer's assistant's face assured him that no immediate harm was meant, and he stood his ground, his eyes flashing, defiantly.

"You didn't expect us to meet quite so soon, did you?" remarked Andrew Dilks with a quiet smile.

"No, I didn't," returned Matt bluntly.

"I suppose you were doing your best to keep out of the way of Gulligan and myself."

"Is Gulligan the man I had the row with?"

"Yes."

"Then you are right. I don't want to get into trouble for nothing. That young lady was not to blame for what happened, and I considered it my duty to take her part."

"Mr. Gulligan was very mad," went on Andrew Dilks, still smiling quietly.

" I can't help that. He ought not to have pitched into me the way he did."

" I agree with you."

At these words, so quietly but firmly spoken, Matt's eyes opened in wonder. Was it possible that the old auctioneer's assistant took his part?

" You agree with me?" he repeated.

" Yes, I agree with you. Gulligan was altogether too hasty—he most generally is," returned Andrew Dilks.

" I'll bet you don't dare tell him that," and Matt grinned mischievously.

" I have just told him."

" What?"

" Yes. I believe that unknown man was entirely to blame. It was a shame the way Gulligan carried on. As soon as you ran out he turned upon me for not stopping you, and we had some pretty hot words."

" Good for you!" cried Matt. " I must thank you, not only for myself, but for Miss Bartlett as well."

" Those hot words have cost me my situation," went on Andrew Dilks more soberly.

Instantly Matt's face fell.

" That's too bad, indeed, it is!" he said earnestly. " Why, I would rather have gone home and got the money to pay for the broken stuff than have that happen."

"It was not altogether on account of the broken piece of bric-a-brac," went on Andrew Dilks. "Gulligan has been angry at me for over two weeks —ever since I wouldn't pass off a counterfeit five-dollar bill he had taken in. I said the bill ought to be burned up, but he wouldn't hear of it."

"But now you are out of a job."

"That's true. But I don't much care. Working for him was not easy, and he never paid me my weekly wages of ten dollars until I had asked for it about a dozen times."

"I thought auctioneers made more than that," said Matt. There was something about Andrew Dilks that pleased him, and he was becoming interested in the conversation.

"Most of them do—a good deal more. But Gulligan considered that he had taught me the business, and that I was still under his thumb."

"Why don't you go in business for yourself? It seems to me it would just suit me," said Matt enthusiastically. "I once passed through the town of Rahway, out in New Jersey, and a fellow not much older than you had a big wagon there, and was auctioning stuff off at a great rate—crockery ware, lamps, albums, razors, and a lot more of goods. They said he had been selling goods there every night for a week."

" Those are the fellows who make money," returned Andrew Dilks. " Here in the city the business is done to death. Give a man a good team of horses and a wagon, and enough money to stock up, and he can travel from place to place and make a small fortune."

" I believe you. Why don't you start out?"

" I haven't enough money, that's the only reason."

" How much would it take ?"

" The price of the turnout, from two hundred dollars up, and about a hundred dollars for stock. You know stock can be purchased as often as desired."

" By crickety ! If I had the money I would go in with you !" cried Matt, caught with a sudden idea. " That sort of thing would just suit me."

" You ? Why I thought you were a city boy, a clerk——"

" So I am. But my Uncle Dan always called me a rolling stone, and that hits it exactly. I am tired of New York, and I would jump at the first chance to get out of it and see some of the country."

" Then you are like me," returned Andrew Dilks warmly. He was quite taken with Matt's candor.

" If I had a turnout I would travel all over the
United States, stopping a week here and a week
there. How old are you?"

" Sixteen."

" I am twenty-one. Do you live with your
parents?"

" No, I am alone here."

" So am I. I used to live in Chicago before all
my folks died. I like your appearance. What is
your name?"

Matt told him, and also gave Andrew Dilks a
brief bit of his history. The auctioneer listened
with interest, and then told a number of things concerning himself. He had been with Caleb Gulligan
four years. He had been sick several times, but,
nevertheless, had managed to save a hundred and
thirty-five dollars."

" I've got seventy-five dollars saved, part of
which I got from other brokers than Mr. Fenton,
for running errands, and so forth," said Matt.
" That and your money would make two hundred
and ten dollars. Couldn't we start out on that?"

" We might," replied Andrew Dilks reflectively.
" You are on your way to work now, are you not?"

" Yes, and I ought to be at the office this minute!"
cried Matt, with a start. " Mr. Fenton will be

tearing mad, I know. But I won't care—that is, if we come to a deal."

"Come and see me this evening, then. I am stopping at the Columbus Hotel, on the Bowery."

"I know the place, and I'll be up at seven o'clock," returned Matt; and on this agreement the two separated.

"My, but I would like to become a traveling auctioneer!" said the boy to himself, as he hurried down Broadway. "I wish I had enough money so that we could go in as equal partners. He seems a first-rate chap in every way, and honest, too, or he would not have gotten into that row over the five-dollar counterfeit."

Matt had lost much time in talking to Andrew Dilks, and now, in order to reach Wall street the quicker, he hopped upon the tail-end of a dray that was moving rapidly toward the Battery.

"Beating the cable cars out of a nickel!" he called to the driver, and that individual smiled grimly, and said nothing.

Less than ten minutes later the boy entered the stock-broker's main office. He was just about to pass into Randolph Fenton's private apartment when the figure of a man moving rapidly down the street attracted his attention. It was the red mustached man who had created the trouble at the auction store.

" Please give these books to Mr. Fenton, and tell him I'll be back shortly," said Matt to the head clerk, and without waiting for a reply he placed his package on a desk, and hurried out of the door after the man.

THE PURSUIT OF A FAMILIAR FACE.   Y.A.

CHAPTER V.

MATT IS DISCHARGED.

WHEN Matt Lincoln reached the pavement he saw that the man he was after had reached Wall street and was turning down toward Water street. The boy started on a run and caught up to the individual just as he was about to descend into an insurance office which was located several steps below the level of the street.

" Hold on there !" cried Matt, and he caught the man by the arm.

" What is it, boy ?" demanded the other, with a slight start at being accosted so unexpectedly.

" I want to see you about that piece of bric-a-brac you broke at the auction store up on Nausau street."

The man's face reddened, and he looked confused.

"I don't—don't know what you are talking about," he stammered.

" Oh, yes, you do," returned Matt coolly. " You tried to let the blame fall on a young lady, but it won't work. You must go back, explain matters, and settle up."

"I'll do nothing of the kind!" blustered the red mustached man. He had recovered from his first alarm. "I know nothing of the affair you have in mind. I have not been near an auction store to-day —for a month, in fact."

"That's a whopper!" exploded Matt. "You were in the place less than an hour and a half ago!"

"Nonsense, boy, you have got hold of the wrong man. Let me go."

"Not much I won't! You are the man, and you can't fool me."

"If you don't let go I'll call a policeman just as sure as my name is Paul Carden."

"I don't care what your name is, you've got to go back and set matters straight."

The man glared at Matt for a moment. Then, without warning, he pushed the boy backward. Matt was standing upon the edge of the steps leading to the insurance office at the time, and he went down with a crash into the wire-netting door, knocking a large hole into it.

Before Matt could recover the man darted down Wall street and around the nearest corner. Matt would have gone after him, but the proprietor of the insurance office came out, and demanded to know what he meant by bursting the wire-netting door in such a rude fashion.

"A man knocked me down the steps," Matt explained. "I hope the door isn't ruined."

"Hardly, but there's a hole in it."

"The wire has broken from under the molding, that is all," said the boy. "Let me see if I can't fix it."

He brought out his penknife, and loosened part of the molding. Then drawing the wire back into place, he tacked the molding fast again; and the door was as good as before.

But all this had taken time, and Matt knew it would now be useless to attempt to follow Paul Carden. He looked around the corner, and seeing nothing of the fellow, retraced his steps to Randolph Fenton's establishment.

"Where in the world have you been so long?" demanded Mr. Fenton, as Matt entered the private apartment. "Here I have been waiting an hour for you to deliver a message to Ulmer & Grant. I hire you to be on hand when wanted, Lincoln; not to loaf your time away."

"I was not loafing my time away, Mr. Fenton," returned Matt calmly. "There was a private matter I had to attend to, and——"

"You have no business to attend to private matters during office hours!" roared Randolph Fenton wrathfully. "You will mind my business and nothing else."

"But this could not wait. There was a man——"

"I do not care for your explanations, young man. Too much time has already been wasted. Take this message to Ulmer & Grant's, and bring a reply inside of ten minutes, or consider yourself discharged."

And with his face full of wrath and sourness, Randolph Fenton thrust a sealed envelope into Matt's hand.

An angry reply arose to the boy's lips. But he checked it, and without a word left the office and hurried away on his errand.

"I trust I make a satisfactory arrangement with Andrew Dilks," said Matt to himself. "It is growing harder and harder every day to get along with Mr. Fenton. Every time he talks he acts as if he wanted to snap somebody's head off. Poor Miss Bartlett at her desk looked half-scared to death."

Arriving at the offices of Ulmer & Grant, Matt found that Mr. Ulmer had gone to Boston. Mr. Grant was busy, but would give him an answer in a few minutes.

Matt sat down, wondering what Mr. Fenton would say about the delay. Ten, fifteen, twenty minutes passed. At last Mr. Grant was at liberty, but it was exactly half an hour before Matt managed to gain a reply to the message he carried.

When Matt got back to Randolph Fenton's office he found the broker in his private apartment alone, and almost purple with suppressed rage.

"You think it smart to keep me waiting, I suppose?" he sneered, as he took Mr. Grant's message and tore it open.

"It was not my fault. Mr. Ulmer is away, and Mr. Grant was busy."

"Why didn't you let Mr. Grant know I was in a hurry?"

"The clerk said he was not to be disturbed just then, and——"

"No more explanations, Lincoln. I took you into this office more for the sake of your poor father than for anything else. But you have not endeavored to make the most of your chances——"

"I have done my work, and more," interrupted Matt bluntly.

"Stop! don't contradict me, young man! You are more of an idler than aught else. This noon you wasted an hour on that errand to Temple Court, and——"

"Mr. Fenton," interrupted a voice from the doorway, and looking up the stock-broker saw Ida Bartlett standing there.

"What is it?" snapped the broker.

"If you please, I would like to say a word in Matthew's behalf," went on the stenographer timidly.

"It's no use saying anything, Miss Bartlett," put in Matt hastily. "Mr. Fenton won't listen to any explanations."

"Yes, but it was——"

"It's no use," went on Matt in a whisper. "I'm not going to stand it any longer," and then he added, as the stock-broker's attention was arrested by the reply Mr. Grant had sent. "I am ready to leave anyway, if he discharges me, and you will only get into trouble if you mention that auction-store affair."

"But it was all my fault——"

"No, it wasn't, and please keep quiet."

"But if you are discharged, Matt——"

"I've got something else in view."

"Oh!"

"Well, what have you to say, Miss Bartlett?" asked Randolph Fenton, tearing up the message and throwing the pieces into the waste basket.

"I—I was going to say that I was partly to blame for his being behind time this noon. I was——"

"Do not try to shield him, Miss Bartlett. I know him better than you do. He is a very lazy and heedless boy, and I have already made up my mind what I am going to do in the matter."

" And what's that?" asked Matt, although he felt pretty certain of what was coming.

" This shall be your last day of service in these offices. This afternoon I will pay you what is due you, and to-morrow I will endeavor to get a boy who is willing to attend to business and not fritter away his time on the streets."

" I have not frittered away my time," replied Matt warmly. "And I feel certain you will not get any one to do more than I have done. You expect a boy to do two men's work for a boy's pay——"

" Stop!"

" Not until I have finished, sir. I am perfectly willing to leave, even though times are dull, and have been contemplating such a step on my own account for some time. I was getting tired of being a slave."

" You outrageous imp! Not another word from you. I will not have you in this place another minute! Go to Mr. Gaston and draw your pay and leave, and never let me see your face again!"

And white with passion, Randolph Fenton sprang to his feet and threw open the door for Matt to pass out.

CHAPTER VI.

A BUSINESS PARTNERSHIP.

Mr. Randolph Fenton's voice had been raised to its highest pitch, and thus the attention of every one in the offices had been attracted to what was going on.

Ida Bartlett again came forward to speak in Matt's behalf, but ere she could say a word the boy put up his hand warningly, and turned to the book-keeper.

"I will take what is due me, Mr. Gaston," he said.

Mr. Gaston, a somewhat elderly man, nodded, and without a word, turned to his desk and passed over to Matt two new one-dollar bills.

"I'm sorry, my boy, it isn't more," he whispered.

"Thank you," returned Matt. "Good-by," he went on, turning to the other office workers. And with a smile and a bow to Ida Bartlett, he passed out of the place.

Not until he was some distance away did he draw a deep breath. Somehow he felt as if he had just emerged from a prison cell.

"It's a wonder to me that I stood it so long," he muttered to himself. "Mr. Fenton is a regular tyrant, and ought to move to Russia. How poor father ever came to invest in those mining shares through him is a mystery to me." Matt gave a sigh, and for an instant an unusually sober look crossed his handsome face. "If only I could learn what became of poor father—if I could make sure whether he was alive or dead—I wouldn't care how other matters went. I must continue my searching as soon as I can afford to do so."

Matt boarded with a private family on Third avenue, and having nothing else to do, he walked slowly to the place. He wished he might meet the man with the red mustache or Andrew Dilks, but he saw nothing of either. When he arrived at the boarding-house it was still an hour to supper-time. He ascended to his room and spent the time in looking over his wardrobe, for Matt was handy with a needle, and disliked to have buttons off or rent seams in his garments.

At length the bell for supper rang, and washing up and combing his hair, he went below. He ate his portion leisurely, and was just finishing when the landlady said there was a young lady to see him in the parlor.

Matt at once thought of Ida Bartlett, who lived but a few blocks away, with her two sisters and her mother. He was right; it was the young lady stenographer.

"I could not wait, Matt, and so came over just as soon as we had tea," she explained. "I want you to tell me what you are going to do, now you are out of Mr. Fenton's offices. You spoke of having something else in view. I trust it is something better."

"I can't tell as to that yet," returned the boy, and then sitting down beside her on the *tête-à-tête*, he told her of Andrew Dilks and the auctioneer's proposition.

"That sounds as if it might be quite a good thing," said Ida Bartlett, when he had finished. "You are sure this Dilks is no sharper? There are lots of sharpers in the auction business, you know."

"Like the one who tried to make you pay?" laughed Matt.

"Exactly."

"Well, to tell the truth, I thought of that. But Dilks doesn't look like a sharper; quite the contrary. Of course, I'll have to keep my eyes open. We will have a written agreement, and I will not let the outfit go out of my sight, at least not until I know him thoroughly."

" In that case I think you will be safe."

" It is possible that we may not come to any agreement. He has more money than I. He may want somebody who can put up an equal amount."

" How much has he ?"

".A hundred and thirty-five dollars."

"And that is a good deal more than you have, I suppose?"

" I have saved seventy-five dollars," returned Matt, and not without some pride.

" Is it possible! And on a salary of four dollars a week !"

" Not much ! That salary only paid my way. I saved the money out of extras I earned from other brokers—running errands for them and doing writing at home in the evenings."

" I see. It is very creditable to you."

" Yet Mr. Fenton said I was lazy," replied Matt bitterly.

" Don't you care what he said. He is a very mean man—I am finding that out more and more every day. I myself intend to leave just as soon as I can find another place. I have been there three months, and can hardly bear it longer."

" The last stenographer only stayed two months,

and the one before that, a man, didn't stay the week out," grinned Matt. "They soon find out what kind of a man he is."

"I would leave to-morrow, only I cannot afford to be out of work, and times are somewhat dull. But, about your proposed venture. You will need sixty dollars more to hold an equal share if you go in, won't you?"

" Yes."

Ida Bartlett meditated for a moment.

"Perhaps I might let you have that money," she said slowly.

"Why—I—I—have you got it?" stammered Matt.

"Yes; I and my two sisters have saved quite a bit out of our earnings, you must know. I'll have to ask Kate and Jennie and mother first. If they are willing, I'll let you have the sixty dollars, and then you and this Dilks can form an equal partnership."

" You are very kind," exclaimed the boy warmly, for the offer was entirely unexpected.

"No more than I ought to be, Matt. You saved me from great annoyance this noon, and I have not forgotten the many favors you have done me from time to time. When did you say you were to **meet** this Dilks?"

"This evening. I ought to be on my way to his hotel now."

"Then do not let me detain you longer."

"I guess he'll wait."

"I will speak to my two sisters and my mother to-night, and I will let you know to-morrow what they think of the matter. If they do not consent, I can let you have twenty-five dollars on my own account, anyway."

"Thank you. But, supposing the venture doesn't pay? We may go all to pieces on the road."

"I'll risk that—with you," smiled Ida Bartlett. "If you cannot make it pay in one place, I know you'll soon find some other place where it will pay. The main thing is to make sure that this Andrew Dilks is honest. I would not like to hear of you being swindled."

"Nor would I want to be swindled," smiled Matt. "It wouldn't pay, and, besides, I might find it a hard job to pay back what I had borrowed."

"You may make a fortune!"

"I would be content if we made a good living."

"And you would be able to see a good part of the country."

"That's the best part of it—to me. I hate to stay in one place all the while. Besides "—Matt lowered his voice—"it will give me a chance to look for my father, if he is still alive."

"You poor boy," returned Ida Bartlett sympathetically. "Always thinking of him! Well, I trust, with all my heart, that you may some day find your father, alive and well."

CHAPTER VII.

GETTING READY TO START.

A few minutes later found Matt on his way to the Columbus Hotel. The Bowery was crowded with all classes of people, some just returning from work, and others out sightseeing and buying, but the boy had no difficulty in making his way along at a rapid gait. In less than a quarter of an hour he reached the hotel and entered the office. He was about to accost the clerk at the desk, when somebody tapped him on the shoulder, and turning he saw Andrew Dilks.

"I have been watching for you," said the young man. "I was a little afraid you might disappoint me."

"I was detained," said Matt. "But I am at your service now. Where shall we go?"

"My room is rather small and warm, but it is more private than the reading-room down here," returned Andrew Dilks. "Suppose we go up there.

You can sit by the window and get what little breeze there is."

They started for the stairs (there was no elevator, as in all better-class hotels), and were soon comfortably seated in Andrew Dilks' room, an apartment on the third floor, in the rear.

"It's not a very elegant place," remarked the young man apologetically, "but it's cheap, and that's what I wanted. A fellow can't spend his money and save it, too."

"You are right there."

"As I said before, old Gulligan only gave me ten dollars a week, and out of that I had to pay for many articles that got broken. He put off what he could on me, whether it was my fault or not."

"I believe you said you had a hundred and thirty-five dollars?"

"Yes. It's not much, but it's something. I wish you had as much. I've figured it that we might start with a single horse and an ordinary covered wagon on two hundred and seventy dollars, and still keep twenty dollars in cash for emergencies."

"I have an idea I can raise the amount."

"You can? Good enough!"

"But, first, I want you to give me some of the particulars of your scheme."

"I'll do that willingly. I want you to understand

every detail before you invest. Then you will know just what to expect."

Andrew Dilks brought out a sheet of paper and a pencil and began to do some figuring.

"We will put down our combined capital at two hundred and fifty dollars," he said. "Now, what can we get a good horse for?"

"Two hundred dollars!" laughed Matt.

"You are right, but we must get one cheaper."

"Supposing we look around for a bargain at one hundred dollars, then?"

"That is nearer the figure. We do not want a fancy animal nor a particularly fast one. A horse that can pull our wagon ten to twenty miles a day once or twice a week will answer."

"Yes; we can trade him off for something better later on."

"Now, I'll put down a hundred for the horse. The wagon ought not to cost over fifty or sixty dollars."

"Make it seventy-five for wagon and harness," said Matt.

"It will foot up to two hundred with rubber blankets and extras."

"I suppose it will. Well, even that will leave us with fifty dollars for stock."

"Will that be enough?"

"We'll make it do. If we run out I can leave you with the turnout, and come back to New York and buy more, and have it shipped as freight to the nearest railroad station."

"I see. I suppose they do not do any trusting with auctioneers?"

"Not with such traveling auctioneers as we will be. I would rather buy for cash, anyway, for you can buy much cheaper."

"I suppose you can. What would you take along, and where would you go?"

"My idea for the balance of this summer would be to strike out through New York State down into Pennsylvania, and then across to New Jersey. Then we can rent a store in some small town for the winter, especially for the holidays, and start out early in the spring for the New England States."

This plan met with Matt's approval, and he asked what goods Andrew Dilks thought would be the most profitable to take along.

"I have a list here in my pocket," returned the young man, bringing it forth. "You see, it includes fancy articles and statuary, besides cheap watches, table cutlery, spoons, imitation gold rings, such musical instruments as accordions, banjos and violins, albums, razors, whips, and a dozen others. That ought to meet the wants in almost any small town."

"Can you play the musical instruments?" asked Matt.

"I can play the accordion—not very well, but enough to show the instrument off."

"I can play the banjo, and also the harmonica. You had better lay in a stock of mouth harmonicas."

"I certainly will if you can play them. They will sell readily if they are shown off. It is good you can play the banjo. We can play that and the accordion whenever we want to open up, and thus attract a crowd. Some use a bell, but music, even when it is poor, is better. Sometimes I used to sing a comic song or two for old Gulligan when we were on the road, but I didn't much care to do it."

"No, I wouldn't like that," said Matt.

"Gulligan sold lots of what are called 'fake' goods," went on Andrew Dilks. "But my intention is to sell honest goods and sell them for just what they are. We will perhaps not make as much, but people will be better pleased, and they will not want to run us out of town if we ever go back to the same place again."

"I am with you there," said Matt heartily. "I was afraid you might want to palm off a lot of trash for first-class goods and I didn't want to be a party to any such transaction."

They continued to talk the subject over for fully

an hour, and by that time both understood each
other thoroughly, and had decided, if Matt could
raise the necessary cash, to go into the scheme
without delay.

" You see, we ought to do all the traveling
possible before cold weather sets in," said Andrew
Dilks. " It is in the villages where the most money
is to be made, especially now, when the farmers are
about done harvesting and have some ready cash."

" As I am out of work, I can start the moment I
get the money," said Matt. " And even if I don't
get that other money, I am willing to put in every
cent of what I have now."

On the following morning Matt was surprised to
receive another visit from Ida Bartlett, who had
eaten an unusually early breakfast so that she might
come over before going to work.

" I knew you would be anxious to hear from me,"
she said. " It is all right. The others are willing
to let you have the money for a year at the regular
bank interest, three per cent.

" Thank you, and I'll try to pay it back before
the year is out," returned Matt, much relieved.

" And you have arranged to go into the scheme?
It is all satisfactory ?"

" Yes."

" Good ! I wish you every success."

CHAPTER VIII.

AN UNEXPECTED SET-BACK.

THE next three days were busy ones for Matt and his newly-made partner. After they had drawn up and signed such papers as they deemed proper between themselves, they set out to look for a horse and wagon.

Andrew Dilks had cut several advertisements of bargains from the morning papers, and these they hunted up one after another.

The so-styled bargains proved to be more or less false. In nearly every instance they ran across some shrewd horse-dealer, who, under pretense of selling an outfit for a widow, or man who had left the city, tried to palm off on them an animal and wagon not worth taking away.

Late in the afternoon, however, when they were almost ready to give up and go to a regular dealer, they ran across a German baker who was selling out at a private sale.

"I vos go to Chermany next veek," he explained

to the two. " Mine old fadder vos dead, and he vos left me all his land and houses in Bremen. See, I vos shown you der letter from der lawyers vot have his vill got."

And he produced a large letter-head, upon which was written a dozen lines in German, which neither could read.

" Never mind that." said Andrew. "Show us your horse and wagon, and set a bottom cash price on them."

" Come dis vay."

The baker led the way around the corner to a boarding-stable, and brought forth a good, chunky brown-and-white horse, that did not look to be over six years old.

" Stand around, Billy !" he cried. " Dere he vos, chentlemen, and chust so goot a horse as der vos in New York."

" Anything the matter with him?" asked Matt, as he began an examination of the animal.

" Not a ding, sir. He vos sound as a tollar, and chentle as a lamb. I vos use him on der bread route for a year and more."

" And where is the wagon?" questioned Andrew Dilks.

" Here vos der wagon," said the baker, as he ran the vehicle out so that they might look it over.

It was a four-wheeled affair, quite large and
heavy. There was one seat in the center, and before and behind this were two big boxes, each with
a hinged lid. In the rear was a rack for pies and
cakes. There was also a box under the seat, and a
money drawer which opened with a concealed push
button.

" This is just the thing for us," whispered Andrew
to Matt. " For a one-horse wagon, it could not be
better arranged. The running gear seems to be in
good condition, too."

" Vell, vot you dinks of them?" asked the baker,
after they had finished their survey.

" Where is the harness?" asked Matt.

" Here she vos, new two veeks ago, and here vos
der vip, too."

" And what is the lowest you can take for the
rig?" asked Andrew. " We are willing to pay spot
cash, but cannot afford a fancy figure."

" I vos sold der whole dings for dree hundred
dollar."

At this announcement Matt's face fell. Three
hundred dollars! It was more than they had to
spend for both turnout and stock.

" Three hundred dollars," repeated Andrew
Dilks. " If that's the case, we can't do business
with you."

"Dot's too pad. How much you gif, hey?"

"We will give you a hundred and seventy-five."

At this announcement the German baker held up his hands in horror, and muttered a number of ejaculations in his native tongue.

"Make it two hundred and seventy-five," he said.

"We can't do it."

"Den take der turnout for two hundred and fifty."

"No, we can't do it," said Matt, and with a wink to Andrew Dilks, he pulled his companion toward the stable doors.

"Hold up!" shouted the baker, in alarm. "Don't go yet, chentlemen. Make dot figure two hundred and twenty-five, and it vos more as tog cheap at dot."

"Perhaps it is, but we can't afford to pay it."

"If I could haf der dime to sell, I vos got more as dot, chentlemen."

"Perhaps so," returned Matt. "But you haven't got to accept our offer, you know. We'll look around for something cheaper."

"You vill bay cash on der spot?"

"Yes; but you must give us a free and clear bill of sale."

"I vos do dot. Make it chust two hundred dollar."

But Andrew Dilks had set his mind on getting a further reduction, and at last the bargain was settled, and they paid over a hundred and ninety dollars for the turnout, leaving them still ten dollars to expend upon rubber blankets and other necessary articles.

The purchase completed, they made arrangements with the boarding-stable keeper to keep the horse and wagon for them until the following Monday morning. In the meantime they procured some paint, and painted over the baker's signs on the wagon, and then Andrew, who was a fair letterer, painted on each side of the wagon-cover the following:

THE EUREKA AUCTION COMPANY.
Best and Cheapest Goods on Earth.

"There, that ought to attract attention wherever we go," said Andrew when the job was finished. "The word company makes it sound big, and we can call ourselves a company as well as not."

On Friday and Saturday the two made a tour of the wholesale houses in New York, and Andrew expended the fifty dollars as judiciously as possible in the purchase of goods. As business was rather slow, and ready money scarce, he struck several decided bargains, especially in cutlery and musical instruments. He had all of the goods sent up to the stable, and the two worked until ten o'clock Saturday night stowing away all of the stock in their wagon.

"Now, we are all ready for the start on Monday morning," said Andrew as the two walked away from the stable.

"Yes, but we haven't decided where we shall go first yet," returned Matt.

"Let us leave that until the last minute. We know about where we are going, and it doesn't make much difference what villages we strike so long as we do the business."

Sunday passed quickly enough for Matt. He attended church and the Sunday-school into which Ida Bartlett had introduced him, and in the evening he packed his valise with all of his worldly possessions. Ida Bartlett also came over to bid him good-by, and remained to give him such advice as he might have received from an elder sister.

Matt had arranged to meet Andrew at the stable at six o'clock sharp, and quarter of an hour before the appointed time found him on his way to the place, valise in hand.

"I'll show Andrew that I mean to be on time," he thought to himself, as he turned into the street upon which the stable was situated.

Suddenly he saw a crowd running up from the block below. There were at least a dozen men and boys, some of whom were shouting at the top of their lungs :

"Fire! fire!"

"Fire!" repeated Matt quickly. "I wonder where it can be?"

But hardly had he uttered the words than, happening to glance toward the stable in which their turnout was located, he saw a thick volume of smoke come pouring out of several of the upper windows.

"My gracious!" he gasped, his face blanching. "It's that stable, and our horse and wagon with the stock still inside!"

"That place is doomed!" said a man beside Matt. "See how the fire is gaining headway! They won't be able to save a single horse or anything else!"

CHAPTER IX.

THE RESULT OF A FIRE.

It was no wonder that Matt's heart was filled with dismay when he saw the stable which contained the auction outfit being thus rapidly devoured by the flames. Almost every cent he possessed was invested in the horse, wagon and stock, and if they were consumed he would be left in New York City next to penniless.

Close to where he was standing was a grocery store, and rushing into this he threw his valise on the counter.

"Keep this for me, please!" he cried to the proprietor. "I want to try to save my horse and wagon!"

And before the grocer could reply he was out of the store again, and running toward the burning stable as fast as his feet could carry him.

When he reached the front of the building, which was three stories high, and quite broad and deep, he found an excited mob of stable-hands, cab-drivers

SAVING THE WAGON   Y. A

and tradespeople assembled, each trying to get inside to save his belongings.

The owner of the stable was also present, having just arrived, and was directing, or trying to direct, the movements of the highly excited ones.

"Go into the alley on the left!" he shouted. "You can get more out of the side doors. The smoke is blowing too thickly out here!"

A rush was made for the alley, and Matt got into the midst of the crowd. The side doors, to which the owner of the stable had referred, were found to be securely bolted from the inside.

"Get some axes!"

"Get a log and smash in the doors!"

"Never mind that!" yelled Matt. "I'll climb through one of the windows and open the door!"

"Good for the boy!"

"Give me a boost up, somebody!"

Half a dozen willing hands raised Matt's form to one of the small side windows, and an instant later the boy's form disappeared within the smoke-laden building.

"He can't stand it in there!"

"He'll be smothered to death!"

Once inside, Matt found it advisable to crouch low down to the floor, for the smoke did, indeed, almost smother him. He could see but little, and had to feel his way out of a stall, and across the floor to where the doors he wished to open were located.

" I'm afraid our nag will be a goner!" he thought dismally. " A horse never can stand anything in the shape of a fire."

At last the doors were reached. Fortunately, he found the bolts at once, and lost not a second in drawing them from their sockets. Then he gave the doors a kick outward, and willing hands flung them far back against the side of the building. Then came a rush of men and boys, all eager to save something. For the moment it looked as if Matt would be carried from his feet.

" Here, don't knock me down!" he cried. " Remember, I opened the doors for you."

" So he did!" returned a burly cab driver. " Give the lad a show!"

And then Matt was given room. He quickly found his way through the smoke and heat to where the wagon stood, ready for the start on the road. The horse was but a few feet away snorting in alarm.

Matt had handled horses before, and he now knew just the best possible thing to do. Taking off his coat, he flung it over Billy's head, thus completely blindfolding him. Then he led the animal out of the stall, and started him toward the open doors.

Hi, Matt, is that you?" yelled a voice close at hand.

" Yes, Andy, and I'm glad you have come. See if you can pull the wagon out."

" Can you manage Billy alone?"

" I think I can."

But Matt had his hands full, as he soon learned. Billy was not in the humor to listen and walk the way he desired. He pranced about wildly, and the boy had all he could do to keep from having his feet stepped upon.

But at last Matt managed to reach the open doors, and then he gave the horse a sharp cut on the flank, which sent him up the alley on a canter. The boy did not wait to ascertain how far Billy might continue on his way, but turned swiftly to help his partner, who was straining every nerve to budge the wagon from its resting-place.

" The floor is up-hill to the side doors!" gasped Andrew Dilks. " We can't get it out, I'm afraid!"

" We must get it out!" returned Matt desperately. " Let me get hold of the shafts and you push. And be quick, for the floor overhead looks as if it was going to give away at any minute!"

Andy did as Matt directed, and together they

strained to their utmost. At first the wagon, heavily loaded, refused to budge, but then it moved slowly from its place against the wall.

"Hurrah! we are getting it!" cried Andrew Dilks. "Be sure and guide it right, Matt. Can you see, or is the smoke too thick for you?"

"I can see; but—hold on, or we'll smash into that other wagon."

Matt held back, and allowed another wagon to pass out first. In the meantime, the burning brands from overhead were coming down livelier than ever. One caught Matt on the left arm, burning the flesh slightly, and another landed on Andrew Dilks' neck, causing the auctioneer to howl with sudden pain.

Outside could be heard the whistle of fire-engines and the clanging of hook-and-ladder truck bells. Then came a heavy stream of water from somewhere behind them, nearly lifting Andy from his feet.

But the way was now once more clear, and Matt yelled to his partner to push. Both exerted every nerve, and ten seconds later the wagon rolled out of the open doors, and was guided by Matt up the alley.

"Thank goodness we are out!" panted the boy, as they brought the wagon to a standstill in the midst of half a dozen carriages. "Another minute in there would just about have settled me."

"Yes, it was getting dangerous," returned Andy, with a serious shake of his head, as he tied his handkerchief over his burned neck. "Hark! what is that?"

His words were called forth by a dull boom, which made the soft dirt in the alley quake.

"The upper flooring has come down!" shouted several in the crowd.

"They won't be able to get any more stuff out now!"

"We were just in time," remarked Matt, with a shiver. "Supposing we had been in there when that flooring, with all the burning hay and those sleighs that were stored there, came down!"

"We ought to be very thankful, not only for that, but for being able to save our wagon and our horse. If they had been burned up we would have been next door to beggars!"

"By the way, where is Billy?" cried Matt. "I don't see him anywhere around."

"I'm sure I don't know."

"Stay here with the wagon and I'll hunt him up," replied Matt; and he started off without further delay.

The alleyway had now become so choked up with vehicles, horses, and people that it was with great difficulty that he fought his way through the dense mass out to the next street. Once here, he looked up and down for the horse, but could see nothing of him.

"Did you see anything of a brown and white horse around here?" he asked of a stable-hand standing near.

"Yes; just saw him gallop up the street," was the reply. "You had better jump on a horse-car if you want to catch him."

"You saw him run clean out of sight, then?"

"Yes; he must be halfway up to Harlem by this time."

Matt waited to hear no more, but boarded the first horse-car which came along bound north. He took a position on the front platform, and as they moved along kept his eyes open for a sight of the animal in which he owned a half-interest.

Ten blocks had been passed, and the boy was beginning to grow anxious, when, chancing to look over the fence of a small yard adjoining a black-smith shop, he saw a horse standing tied to a post. A second look convinced him that it was Billy, and he at once leaped from the moving car and hurried toward the place.

"Well, sir, what can I do for you?" asked the blacksmith, a tall, heavy-set fellow, as he left his bellows, where he had been blowing up the fire.

" I'll take my horse, please," returned Matt.

" Your horse? Which horse is that?"

" The runaway you just caught."

" I haven't any runaway," returned the black-smith boldly.

" What?" cried the boy in amazement. " Why, of course you have. He is tied to the post in the yard."

" No runaway here."

" I mean the brown and white horse."

" That horse was just left here to be shod."

For the moment Matt was too dumfounded to speak.

" To be shod?" he said at last. " Who left him here?"

" A colored man. I don't know his name."

" But he is my horse, and he doesn't need shoeing."

" I don't know anything about that," returned the blacksmith darkly. " He was left here and that's all I know about it. You'll have to hunt up the colored man, and fix it up with him if you want the horse."

CHAPTER X.

ON THE ROAD AT LAST.

HAD the blacksmith spoken with more real concern, Matt would have believed what he said, but there was that in the fellow's manner which tended to make the boy suspicious.

"How long ago was it that the colored man left the horse?" he asked, after a pause.

"Not more than an hour ago."

"An hour?"

"About that, as near as I can remember. I've been rather busy this morning."

"That horse did not get away until about fifteen minutes ago," returned Matt coldly.

"Oh, you must be mistaken," returned the blacksmith smoothly.

"No, I am not mistaken," replied Matt, and his tones began to grow sharper. "He just got away from me, after I rescued him from a burning stable. He is my horse, and I intend to take him away."

As Matt spoke he crossed the blacksmith shop to where a doorway led to the little yard beyond.

"Hold up there!" cried the blacksmith roughly. "You are not going out there!"

"Yes, I am, and you can't stop me," returned Matt spiritedly. "I own that horse, or at least I own a half-interest in him, and if you dare to molest me you'll get into trouble."

"Will I?" sneered the blacksmith.

"Yes, you will. If you stop me, I'll call in the police."

At these words the blacksmith's face fell. Evidently he had not anticipated that a mere boy would take such a decided stand.

"Yes, but that colored man—" he began, more mildly.

"If there was a colored man in the case, you can explain matters to suit yourself. As for me, I believe you caught the horse yourself and wanted to do what you could to keep him."

"How dare you!" cried the blacksmith, with a threatening gesture. "Do you take me for a thief?"

"Never mind what I take you for. That is my horse, and I am going to take him away."

And undaunted by the blacksmith's manner, Matt marched out into the yard, and untied Billy, who was covered with sweat, and still trembling from fright.

"It's playing a bold game you are," grumbled the man of the anvil, as the boy led the horse through the blacksmith-shop toward the front door. "I reckon you think you are mighty smart."

"One has to be smart to deal with such a man as you!" retorted Matt. "Had you done the fair thing at the start, I might have rewarded you for stopping the horse, but as it is, I don't believe you deserve a cent."

And with this parting shot, which, by the way was fully deserved by the dishonest blacksmith, Matt sprang upon Billy's back and rode off.

When the boy reached the alleyway again he found that the fire department had gotten the fire under control, and that much of the crowd of people had gone on about their business. In the space around the wagon several cabman were busy getting out their horses and cabs, all thankful that their turnouts and animals had not been consumed by the conflagration, which nad all but leveled the great stable to the ground.

Andy was seated on the wagon, anxiously awaiting his return. While the two harnessed Billy into place, Matt told his partner of the trouble he had experienced.

"That blacksmith meant to bluff you off and keep the horse," said the auctioneer. "If you hadn't come back soon I would have gone off after you."

"Is the wagon damaged?" questioned Matt anxiously.

"Not in the slightest. I have examined everything carefully. And the stock is O. K. too. We can start off just as if nothing had happened."

"But we haven't decided yet as to just where we are to go," returned the boy.

"Oh, that reminds me!" cried Andy. "I meant to tell you before, but the fire drove it clean out of my head. I saw a fellow yesterday who is going to strike out up through Harlem to-morrow. He was going to take the very route I had thought out. So I was going to propose that we take the ferry over to Jersey City, and strike out through New Jersey first."

"Well, one way will suit me just as well as another," returned Matt. "So New Jersey it is."

In less than five minutes later they were ready to start. The owner of the stable, nearly distracted over his loss, was around, and into his hand they thrust the money they owed him. Then Matt procured his valise, and without waiting to be questioned by the police and the firemen any more than was necessary, they drove off.

"Not a very favorable start," was Andy's comment, as the scene of the conflagration was left behind. "But they say 'a bad beginning makes a good ending,' so we ought not to lose heart."

"Lose heart!" cried Matt lightly. "No, indeed! I am thankful we are able to start, even though we do look like a couple of tramps," he added with a grin.

"We'll take a wash-up when we are across the ferry. We'll have lots of time, for we won't be able to do any business to-day. We must get at least twenty or thirty miles from New York before we attempt to open up."

The drive down to Cortlandt street ferry was an uneventful one through the crowded streets. A boat had just come in when they reached the ferry-house, and after paying the fare, they drove upon this, and were soon on their way to the New Jersey shore.

"Do you know the road?" asked Matt, as they tied up upon an open street on the other side, and went into the great ferry-house to wash and brush up.

"I know the roads through Newark and Elizabeth," returned Andrew Dilks. "I think we had better strike along the New Jersey Central Railroad as far as Bound Brook or Somerville, and then strike through Flemington, and across to the Delaware River, and so on into Pennsylvania."

" That suits me," returned Matt.

It was exactly half-past ten o'clock when they left the vicinity of the ferry in Jersey City, and moved off toward the old plank road, so called, which leads to Newark, five miles distant. Both were in excellent spirits, despite the thrilling experience through which they had passed.

" I have here a list of all the articles we have in stock," said Andy, as he set Billy on a brisk trot. " You had better study it. The prices are also put down, and of course, we never will auction a thing off for less, unless it is unsalable otherwise and we wish to dispose of it."

" But supposing a thing is put up and people won't bid above a certain figure?"

" We will buy it in ourselves, or get some one to bid for us, or else refuse to take a bid under a certain sum."

Matt took the sheet of paper, and resting on the box in the back of the wagon, began to study it carefully, and so absorbed did he become that he did not notice when Newark was reached, and was only aroused when Andy drew up in front of a restaurant and asked him if he did not feel like having some dinner.

"You can just bet I do!" exclaimed Matt. "The fire and the drive have made me as hungry as a bear."

The restaurant was not a very large place, and but few customers were present. They ordered what they wished, and it was soon brought to them.

"I didn't want to go to one of those high-toned places where they charge big prices," observed Andy, as he began to fall to. "We can't afford to cut a spread until we see how our venture is going to pan out."

"You are right there," returned Matt. "As it is, I think our supply of cash is getting mighty low."

"I notice the knives and forks are rather rusty here," went on Andy. "I wonder if I can't sell the proprietor some table cutlery? We have some on board that is both cheap and good."

"I'd try it by all means," cried Matt heartily.

So when the meal was concluded Andrew Dilks walked up to the proprietor, who was also cashier, and paid their bill. Then he asked the man if he did not think some new knives and forks would be appreciated by his customers.

"I have do doubt but what they would be," returned the restaurant keeper. "But they cost too much money, and times are rather hard."

"I can sell you some cheap," returned Andy, and he mentioned his price.

The restaurant man smiled.

"Too cheap to be good," he said. "I must have some that will stand the wear."

"Let me show you them. Matt, go out and bring in a few dozen of the No. 23 knives and forks, and also some of the X23 spoons," went on Andy briskly.

Matt at once complied, and his partner continued to talk to the restaurant keeper, thus keeping his attention. When the articles were brought Andy invited the prospective purchaser to make a thorough examination of them.

"Send a couple down to the kitchen and have them scoured. They are triple-plated, and will stand it," he added.

Andy's business-like way pleased the restaurant keeper, and after a little more talk he purchased three dozen each of knives and forks and two dozen spoons.

The price was paid over, and both Andy and Matt were congratulating themselves on their good luck, when a man who had been standing near the window of the restaurant peering in stepped inside and tapped both on the shoulder.

"I would like to see your license for selling," he said sternly.

CHAPTER XI.

HARSH TREATMENT.

Both Matt and Andy were considerably taken aback by the unexpected demand of the stranger. When they had come to Newark they had not expected to sell anything, and therefore had not given the question of a license a single thought.

"Excuse me, but I am sorry to state we have no license," returned Andy frankly. "We did not expect to make any sales here, but were going straight through to Elizabeth."

"Very likely," sneered the man, who was a special officer attached to the police department. "But I saw you make the sale, and you must come with me."

"Oh, Andy, let us pay the license," exclaimed Matt, in a low voice, as visions of a week or a month in jail floated before his mind. It would be simply terrible to be locked up.

"That's what we will have to do," returned Andy,

who had been through such a predicament before,
and was not, therefore, greatly alarmed. "Don't
be afraid; we will come out all right. Only it will
cost us two or three dollars."

"I don't care if it costs fifty—I don't want to run
afoul of the law," returned Matt bluntly.

"Nor do I," returned his partner.

"Well, what do you say?" demanded the officer
sharply.

"We will go with you and pay the license,"
replied Andy.

"All right."

"Will you ride with us?"

"Don't care if I do," said the officer, and all three
hopped on the wagon seat, and Matt drove off.

The office where licenses could be procured was
at the City Hall, on Broad Street. When they turned
into that thoroughfare Matt uttered a cry of surprise.

"What a broad street!" he exclaimed, as he surveyed it.

"It is one of the broadest in any eastern city,"
returned the officer, who seemed inclined to be more
friendly now that they had shown a disposition to
do the right thing.

Inside of the City Hall they were compelled to
wait near half an hour before they could procure

their license. Then they were asked for how long
a term they desired it.

" For to day only," returned Andy, and so it was
made out and as quickly paid for.

"Oh, but I'm glad we are out of that scrape so
easily!" murmured Matt, as the two walked back
to their wagon. " I was afraid they would lock us
up for ten days or a month."

" They would have their hands full locking up
all the peddlers who try to sell goods without a
license," laughed Andy. " All they care for is the
money."

" We will have to pay in almost every town we
go, won't we?"

" Yes, every town. Some places charge so much
that we won't try to sell in them. I'll make it a
point after this to find out about a license as soon
as we enter a place."

" Yes, do that by all means," returned Matt,
much relieved.

Now that they had a license good for the balance
of the day, Matt moved that they remain in Newark
and try to make more sales.

" Let us try all the restaurants," he said. " We
may be able to sell more of those knives and forks
and spoons."

" I am willing," said Andy. " This isn't exactly

auctioneering, but it pays just as well, so we have
no cause to grumble."

They turned back into the business portion of the
city and drove along slowly until two restaurants,
directly opposite to each other, were reached.

" I'll take one and you can take the other," said
Andy. " Be sure and sell all you can," he added,
with a laugh.

Matt nodded, and with half a dozen samples
under his arm, he entered the restaurant on the
right.

It must be confessed that the boy's heart beat
rather fast. This was the first time he had endeavored to effect a sale solely on his own responsibility.
Moreover, Andy was pitted against him, trying to
sell goods in a similar way to similar people.

" I must do as well as he," thought Matt. "If I
don't he may imagine I am not worthy of being an
equal partner in the concern."

The place Matt had entered was handsomely
fitted up in the latest style. It was quite large, but
at this hour of the day was but scantily patronized.
In the back half a dozen waiters were discussing
the merits of certain race horses, while behind the
cashier's desk a young man, with an enormous
diamond, was reading a copy of a sensational weekly.

A waiter rushed forward to conduct Matt to a

seat at one of the tables, but the boy shook his head and turned to the desk.

"Can I see the proprietor?" he asked.

The clerk had laid down his paper and gave Matt an ugly stare before replying.

"So you are another one of them," he said slowly, as he surveyed the boy from head to foot.

Matt was somewhat mystified by this, but smiled pleasantly.

"I suppose I am—if you say so," he said. "Did you say the proprietor was in?"

"No, I didn't say so. Say, you'll wish you hadn't come here if old Mattison gives you a chance," went on the young man, in a lower voice.

"Why will I wish that?" questioned Matt, more mystified than ever.

"Because he's a tough customer to get along with."

"But if my goods and the price suit, why, it ought to be all right."

"Goods and price? What are you talking about?" demanded the young man quickly.

"The goods I have to sell—knives, forks, and spoons."

"Oh, pshaw! I thought you were another of those chumps that want my place here. Old Mattison gave me notice to quit next Saturday, and put an advertisement in the paper for a new clerk, and there have been about a dozen here already."

" And none of them suit?"

" Suit! He's a man that is never suited."

" Then perhaps I won't be able to sell him any goods," returned Matt, his heart sinking.

" It ain't likely. Business is poor, and he ain't buying more than he can help. You can try him, though."

" Where is he?"

" I'll call him."

The young man behind the desk rang the bell for one of the waiters, and sent that individual upstairs for the proprietor. The waiter was gone nearly five minutes before he returned, accompanied by a short, stout man, with bushy black hair and a heavy beard.

" Well, sir, what can I do for you?" asked the man of Matt.

" If you are not too busy I would like to show you some goods which are both good and very cheap," returned Matt, as easily as he could, and without waiting for a reply he unrolled his package of samples, and placed them upon the desk.

" And is that what you called me downstairs for?" cried the proprietor of the restaurant, in a rage. ' Make me throw down a good hand at cards just to look at a lot of tin knives and forks! You peddlers are getting more bold every day. The police ought to sit down on every one of you!"

" I am sorry if I disturbed your leisure," returned Matt, as mildly as he could. " But, I thought——"

" You thought you would just like to cheat me into buying a lot of your trash," finished the restaurant proprietor. " Well, you can't do anything of the kind, and you can take that for your impudence!"

And hastily gathering up the package of samples, the restaurant keeper walked to 'the open doorway and flung knives, forks and spoons into the muddy gutter!

CHAPTER XII.

MATT STANDS UP FOR HIMSELF.

It was evident, by the self-satisfied look upon the restaurant-keeper's face, that the hot-tempered man supposed that he had done a very smart thing in thus disposing of Matt's wares by throwing the bundle into the muddy gutter of the street.

"Now pick up your goods and skip out!" he cried, as he turned to the boy. "And the next time you be careful how you disturb folks when they are trying to take it a little easy!"

For the instant Matt was stupefied, and stood still, hardly moving a muscle.

Then the boy's natural temper arose to the surface, and for the moment he felt as if he must fly at the man and pound him in the face just as hard as he could. His face grew first red and then deadly pale. The man saw the change in his countenance, saw the fire flash in the boy's eyes, and stopped short just as he was about to repeat his injunction to leave the establishment.

" You are a—a brute !" exclaimed Matt, stepping forward with clinched fists.

" What's that ?" cried the restaurant-keeper, so loudly that several customers and a number of the waiters gathered round to learn the cause of the trouble.

" I say you are a brute !" repeated Matt, undaunted by the fierce look the restaurant-keeper had assumed. " If you did not wish to buy from me you could have said so. There was no need for you to throw my goods in the gutter."

" Shut up and clear out !" growled the man. " I want no back talk from the likes of you. Do you suppose I buy from beggars and thieves ?"

" I am neither a beggar nor a thief !" returned Matt striding still closer. " And I won't allow you nor any one else to say so."

" Oh, you won't ?" sneered the man.

" No, I won't," answered Matt firmly. " My business is just as honest and honorable as yours, even though I may not make such enormous profits," he added, bound in some way to " get square."

" See here, are you going to get out, or must I pitch you out ?" howled the man more savagely than ever.

For the moment Matt did not reply. He was

very angry, but knew it would do him more harm
than good to lose his temper. Yet he was not the
person to allow the insults he had received to pass
unnoticed.

" I will get out just as soon as you restore my
goods to me," he said. " You had no right whatever to throw them into the gutter and soil
them."

" What ?"

" And let me say, too, that I expect my goods to
come back to me just as clean as they were when
you took them."

" You say another word and I'll stand you on
your head!" fumed the proprietor of the restaurant,
but the look in Matt's eyes kept him from laying
hands upon the boy.

" If you dare to touch me I'll call in the police,"
replied Matt, more sharply than ever. " I have a
license, and by that license the police are bound to
protect me. Now, you get my goods back for me
and I'll leave."

" I'll see you in Jericho first !"

" Very well; but remember, if anything is lost or
damaged, you'll pay the bill."

" Good for the boy !" exclaimed one of the men
who had just been lunching in the place. " I like
to see a fellow stick up for his rights."

" See here, I want no outside interference here!"
blustered the restaurant-keeper. " I am fully ca-
pable of attending to this affair myself."

" Well, I'm going to see that the boy gets a
show," returned the other coolly, as he paid the
amount of his check and lit a cigar taken from his
pocket. " I don't think it was a fair deal to throw
his stuff in the gutter."

" It wasn't," put in another customer. " He's got
to make a living, just the same as all of us."

" Oh, don't talk!" cried the restaurant-keeper, wav-
ing them away with his hand. " Come, now, no
more talk!" he went on to Matt. " Go, before I
have you thrown out."

" I won't budge a step, excepting it is to call the
police," returned Matt, more firmly than ever, now
that he saw he had friends in the crowd. " I'll
give you just five minutes to give me back my
goods."

The restaurant-keeper began to bluster and
threaten, and even sent a waiter out, ostensibly to
call in a policeman. But Matt was not frightened,
and in the end another waiter was sent to gather up
the sample goods, wipe them off and restore them to
the boy.

" Good for you, boy!" said one of the customers,
as he followed Matt out upon the sidewalk. " Al-

ways stick up for your rights," and he nodded pleasantly and passed on.

When Matt reached the wagon he found Andy had not yet come back. He accordingly looked around, and seeing another restaurant about half a block further down the street entered it.

He found the proprietor behind the desk, laughing quietly to himself. He had heard of what had happened in his neighbor's place, and was immensely tickled thereby.

" Hullo! ain't you the boy that had the row with Mattison?" he exclaimed in surprise.

" I had some trouble with that man," said Matt. " But it was not my fault, I can assure you."

" You came out ahead, didn't you? Ha! ha! ha! It does me good to hear it. Tell me how the row started."

Matt did so, and was compelled to go into all the details, to which the man listened with keen interest.

" Served him right! He can get along with nobody. But you are a clever one, too."

" Thank you," replied Matt.

And then he began to talk business, showing up his somewhat bedimmed samples to the best possible advantage, and quoting prices in a manner that made the restaurant-keeper think he was an old hand at the business.

The man was not particularly in need of anything, but he liked Matt's way, and thought it was
worth something to have a good story to tell to his
rival's discredit. He bought four dozen triple-
plated spoons and a carving-knife, and then Matt
persuaded him to invest in a new toothpick holder,
and a match holder of aluminum, which were both
very pretty and cheap.

"Just an even seven dollars!" thought Matt, as
he hurried back to the wagon. "I don't think that
so bad. Our profits on that sale ought to be at
least two dollars."

Andy was waiting for him. He had sold, after a
good deal of hard talking, a dozen knives and forks,
upon which he had been forced to make a slight
discount. He listened to Matt's story in amazement.

"Seven dollars' worth! That's fine, Matt! You
must be a born salesman. Keep right on, by all
means."

"But I don't expect any such luck every time,"
returned the boy, and then he told the story of his
troubles in the first restaurant he had visited.

"It was plucky in you to stick out as you did,"
was Andy's comment. "I don't believe I could
have done it. I would have gone out and picked up
the things myself."

"I wouldn't, never!" cried Matt, and his whole face showed the spirit within him.

It was only four o'clock in the afternoon, and Andy suggested that they continue to try their luck until sundown. So they drove on down the street slowly, visiting every restaurant and many stores on the way.

In one place Matt sold a dozen spoons, and in another a fancy water-pitcher. Andy sold some spoons also, and a cheap watch and chain, which the buyer explained he intended to sell to some customer for double the money.

At the last place at which they stopped Andy made arrangements to remain all night. A stable was also found for Billy and the wagon, and by eight o'clock the partners found themselves free from business cares. Matt moved that they have supper, and to this Andy willingly agreed.

While the two were waiting for their orders to be filled, Andy brought out a bit of paper and a pencil and began to figure.

"The net receipts for the day were eighteen dollars and a half," he said, when he had finished. "The goods and the license cost thirteen dollars and sixty cents. That leaves a profit of four dollars and ninety cents, which is not so bad, considering that we only worked about five hours all told."

"And what were our expenses?" asked Matt.

Andy did a little more figuring.

" Expenses from this morning until to-morrow morning, including this supper, about two dollars and thirty cents."

" Then we have two dollars and sixty cents over all?"

" Yes, that is, without counting wear and tear on wagon, harness, and so forth."

"Of course.   But that isn't so bad."

" Indeed it is not," returned Andy.   " If we do as well as that every day we shall get along very well, although I trust to do even better."

CHAPTER XIII.

THE CORN SALVE DOCTOR.

AFTER supper the two partners found that time hung a little heavily upon their hands. Matt suggested that they walk around the city a bit, taking in the sights, but Andy was too tired.

"I'll tell you what I will do, though," said the older member of the firm. "I'll get one of the accordions out and you can get a banjo, and we can practice a little. There is nothing like being prepared for an emergency, you know."

"That is true, and we'll have to brush up quite a bit if we wish to play in public," laughed Matt.

He accompanied Andy to the barn where the wagon was stored, and they brought not only the accordion and the banjo, but also a violin and a mouth harmonica.

These instruments they took to the bedroom which had been assigned to them, and here, while it was yet early, they tuned up and began to practice upon such simple tunes as both knew by heart.

Matt first tried the banjo, and after he had it in tune with the accordion, the partners played half a dozen selections quite creditably.

" We wouldn't do for grand opera soloists, but I guess it will be good enough to attract crowds in small country towns," laughed Andy, as he ground out a lively German waltz.

" Supposing we try the violin and banjo," suggested Matt, and Andy took up the king of instruments.

But this did not go so well, and it was not long before Andy turned back to the accordion, which, according to his statement, half-played itself. Matt tried the mouth harmonica, and surprised not only Andy, but half a dozen listeners, by the wonderful effects he produced upon the little instrument.

" Good for you !" shouted Andy, as Matt finished a particularly clever selection. " If the auction business fails, you can go on the variety stage."

" No, thank you," returned Matt. " I understand enough about it to know that it is little better than a dog's life. I just as lief stick to what I'm doing, or become a traveling order salesman for some big New York house."

" Well, I don't know but what that shows your level-headedness," returned Andy.

The two slept soundly that night. Matt was up

at five o'clock the next morning, and he at once aroused his partner. They had an early breakfast, and then walked around to the stable where the wagon was housed.

While they were hitching up Billy a middle-aged man, rather slouchy in appearance, came shuffling in.

"Are you the two young fellers what's running this here auction wagon?" he began, addressing Matt.

"We are," returned the boy. "What do you want?"

"Pretty good business, ain't it?" went on the stranger, without answering the question which had been put.

"Sometimes it is."

"I reckon there's a heap of money in it," proceeded the shabby stranger.

"Well, we are not yet millionaires," put in Andy, with a pleasant laugh.

"I know a feller what made a pile of money in the auction business," remarked the man as he ejected a quantity of tobacco juice from his mouth. "He was a rip-snorter at it, though—could talk a table into walking off—and keep it up all day and half the night."

To this statement Matt and Andy made no reply.

Neither liked the looks of the newcomer, and both wished he would go away.

"Say, you don't want to take a fellow in, do you?" asked the man, after a slight pause, as he came close beside Matt, who was nearest to him.

"No, we haven't any work for an outsider" returned the boy.

"I'm a rustler when I get a-going, let me tell you. I can tell stories and sing and sell more goods than any one has any idea of. Besides that, I've got a new corn salve I put up myself which goes like hot cakes. Barberry's Lightning Salve, I call it—my name is Paul Barberry, you know—Dr. Barberry, most of 'em call me. Say the word, and I'll go with you and put up my salve against your outfit, and we'll share and share alike."

"As I said before, we have no room for an outsider," returned Matt, while Andy nodded approvingly. "The wagon seat only holds two, and besides, our plans are all completed for our trip."

"Humph!" The man's face took on a sour look. "You are missing the chance of your lives."

"We'll risk it," laughed Andy.

"I can sell more salve than you can sell other goods every day in the week—and make more money, too."

"Then you had better start alone—and at once," returned Andy shortly.

"I will—if you fellers won't take me in as a working partner. I made the suggestion only because I thought it would be more pleasant to travel in a company of three."

"We are satisfied to go it without outside assistance," cried Matt, as he hopped on the seat. "All ready, Andy?"

"Yes, go on," returned his partner, climbing up beside him.

"Then you won't make a deal with me?" questioned Paul Barberry more sourly than ever.

"No," replied Matt and Andy in a breath, and while one gathered up the lines the other spoke to the horse, and the turn out began to leave the stable.

"All right," shouted Paul Barberry. "You may be sorry for it. You young fellows think you know it all, but you may get tripped up badly before long," and picking up an ancient and decidedly rusty traveling-bag which he possessed, the corn salve doctor trudged away up the street.

"What a forward man!" exclaimed Matt, as they moved off. "Why, he actually wanted to force himself on us!"

"There are a good many such fellows on the

road," returned Andy. "The moment they see some one who appears to be prospering, they try their best to get in with him. I dare say that Dr. Paul Barberry is about broke, and would consider it a windfall of fortune to be taken in by the owners and managers of the Eureka Auction Co."

"I wonder if we'll meet him again," mused Matt, as he looked back just in time to see the shabby figure disappear around a corner.

"Oh, he may turn up again; such fellows very often do," replied Andy.

But neither he nor Matt dreamed of the peculiar circumstances under which they would again come in contact with Paul Barberry.

The day was warm and bright, and Billy, the horse, appeared in excellent spirits by the way he trotted along over the macadamized road from Newark to Elizabeth.

It was not their intention to stop at the latter place, but just as they reached the outskirts of the city Billy began to limp, and they saw that one of his shoes had become loose.

"We'll have to take him around to a blacksmith shop," said Andy, and they accordingly drove on until such a place was reached.

Here they found they would have to wait until

dinner-time before the shoe could be refitted. Rather than go to the trouble and expense of getting a license, however, they decided to spend the time in walking around.

"This is one of the oldest towns in New Jersey," remarked Andy, as they walked around the depots and down Broad Street, the main thoroughfare. "Down along the water front is one of the largest sewing machine factories in the world I was through it once and I can tell you it was a sight well worth seeing."

Just before twelve o'clock they stopped in a restaurant not far from the blacksmith shop, and had dinner. By the time this was over Billy's shoe had been readjusted, and once more they were off.

It was easy driving along the smooth country road, and after passing through Cranford, Westfield and several smaller places, they struck out for Plainfield, which Andy declared was to be their first regular stopping place.

"It is a fair-sized city," he said. "And if we can strike the right stand we ought to do well there for several days or a week."

"I hope we do well," returned Matt. "We need a good start, for as yet our ready funds are rather low."

"You will have your first chance to do a bit of

regular auctioneering," smiled Addy. "I trust you
are not nervous over the prospects."

"Never mind if I am," returned Matt bravely.
"I am going to do my best. If I get nervous I'll
get over it just as quickly as I can."

Some time before sundown they entered Plainfield; half an hour later they found a suitable stopping place, and then Andy went off to secure some
stand where they might do business.

He came back in an hour and stated that he had
secured an empty store, which would be much
better than selling from the wagon.

"The store will only cost us a dollar a day as
long as we use it, and we ought to be able to make
that much more out of it," he said.

They went to work that night transferring the
stock from the wagon to the store shelves, and when
this was finished both set to work to wash and dress
the show window.

On the following morning at ten o'clock, they
hung out a red flag, and then the Eureka Auction
Co. was ready for business.

CHAPTER XIV.

THE YOUNG AUCTIONEER.

" I FEEL like a cat in a strange garret !" exclaimed
Matt, as he walked up and down behind the counter
on a raised platform he and Andy had placed there.
" This is like going into cold water an inch at a
time.   I would rather plunge in head first."

" Then here goes," cried Andy, catching up an
accordion that stood close at hand. " Let us see
what we can do toward drawing a crowd in.   There
must be something going on, for the streets are
filling up with people."

" There is a cheap circus to exhibit.   I saw the
posters.   Perhaps they intend to give a parade."

" Most likely.   Get your banjo, Matt, and let us
give them our best selection."

Matt did as requested ; and as the music rang
out those on the pavement began to pause, and
half a dozen stopped at the open door and peered
in.

" Come right in !   Come right in !" shouted Andy.

" The auction is now about to begin, and you don't want to miss the chance of your lives!"

" Plenty of room for everybody!" shouted Matt directly after him. His voice was a trifle unsteady through excitement. "Don't wait outside, but secure a good place, where you can hear and see all that is going on. You need not buy if you do not wish. One more tune, ladies and gentlemen, and then we will show you the best bargains ever exhibited in this city. That's right, come right in!"

Thus urged, the folks began to drift in, singly and in pairs, until, when the next tune was finished, the store held perhaps twenty-five men, women and boys. Several children had tried to enter, but Andy had shook his head at them, and thus kept them outside.

" Say, what's them pocket-knives worth?" asked one old man evidently from the country, as he pointed to a board stuck full of the glittering blades.

" Which knife, sir?" asked Matt, in a business-like way.

" That one with the buckhorn handle and prunin' blade."

" That sir, is one of our best knives. Well made, of the best steel, and one that ought to last you a good many years. What do you offer for it, sir?"

"Offer?" repeated the old man in astonishment.

"Yes, sir, make an offer, please."

"Ain't you got no price sot on it?"

"No, sir; this is an auction store, and we take what we can get for a thing. Come, make an offer."

"I'll give ye a quarter for it," said the old man after considerable hesitation.

"A quarter I am offered for this beautiful knife!" shouted Matt, taking up the blade and holding it up so that all might see it. "It is a knife with four strong blades, a buckhorn handle, well riveted, and extra-tempered springs, fully warranted. A quarter, ladies and gentlemen; who says thirty cents?"

"Thirty!" returned a young man, after an examination of the knife.

"Thirty cents I am offered. Thirty! thirty! Some one make it thirty-five——"

"Thirty-five cents!" put in the old countryman. "I guess that knife is wuth that to me."

"Forty!" said the young man promptly. He appeared to be rich, and was bidding more to tease the old countryman than because he desired the knife.

"Forty I am offered!" sang out Matt, who did

THE YOUNG AUCTIONEERS AT WORK.   Y. A.

not care who obtained the knife, so long as a good figure was reached. "Forty! forty! Come, gentlemen, a bit higher than that, please!"

"Forty-five cents, and that's more than a good price," grumbled the old countryman, who had, however, set his heart on the knife the moment he had first seen it.

"Half a dollar!" sang out the young man promptly.

"Fifty cents I am offered!" went on Matt, in a business-like way. "Fifty cents, gentlemen, for a knife that ought to be in every one's pocket—a knife worth having! Who says seventy-five!"

Matt knew very well that no one in the crowd would make such a jump, but he hoped to cause the old man to bid again, and his hope was realized. Instead of going to fifty-five, the countryman offered sixty cents.

He had hardly made the offer when the young man, thinking he had aroused the old man to a state of recklessness in which he would keep on bidding, offered seventy-five cents for the knife.

"Seventy-five cents I am offered!" cried Matt. "Who makes it a dollar—ninety—eighty-five—eighty?" and he glanced inquiringly at the old countryman.

But the old man shook his head.

"Not a penny over seventy-five cents," he muttered in a low tone.

"Seventy-five!" went on Matt. "Come, now, raise it just a bit! The knife is really worth it. Who says eighty? Seventy-five-five-five! Last call, remember! Going, going—gone! to that young man for seventy-five cents!"

And Matt held out the knife to the last bidder, and motioned to Andy to collect the money.

The young man grew red and drew back.

"Oh, pshaw! I didn't want the knife!" he grumbled. "Put it up again, maybe you'll get a bigger price for it," and he began to edge his way toward the door.

"Hold on! Not so fast!" said Andy, in a low voice, as he caught him by the arm. "This company doesn't do business that way. If you did not wish the knife you should not have bid for it. We are not running this store for fun."

The young man looked at him impudently. But the clear, stern eyes of Matt's partner made him wilt, and muttering something under his breath about getting square, he paid over the amount, took the knife, and sneaked out of the now crowded store.

In the meantime, the old countryman was about to leave, disappointed over his failure to secure the prize he coveted. He wished just such a knife, and knew that he would have to pay a dollar or more at the hardware store for it.

"Wait a minute, please," said Matt to him. "I have another such a knife. If you wish it you can have it at the same figure that the young man paid."

"Let's look at the knife."

The countryman made a careful examination of the blade, and finally agreed to take it.

"I'll send my son Tom around for an accordion," he said, before leaving. "He's dead stuck on music, Tom is."

"Thank you, we shall be pleased to see him," returned Matt politely, and the old countryman went off much pleased over the way he had been treated.

At a word from Andy, Matt brought the entire board of knives out so that all might examine them.

"Seventy-five cents was the auction price," he explained. "So any one can step up and take his or her choice for that amount. They are well worth your inspection. Any of the knives will stick, but you can't get stuck on a single one of them."

This little joke made the crowd laugh, and a dozen or more pressed forward to look at the knives.

One young man bought a pearl-handled article, and a young lady bought one which contained a lead pencil and a button-hook.

While Matt was making these sales Andy was busy showing off the merits of several articles of bric-a-brac which a bevy of ladies were admiring. He told them how he had obtained them at a sacrifice sale, and was thus enabled to sell them quite reasonable. The lady who led the party did not wish to bid on the articles at auction, so Andy very obligingly set a figure, and after some little haggling, the lady took three dollars' worth of goods, to be delivered at her house on the outskirts of the city.

By this time both of the young auctioneers were certain that they were going to have a good day's sales.

"That circus has brought the people out," whispered Andy to Matt. "We were very fortunate to strike here when we did. We must make the most of the day."

"What shall I try next?" asked Matt. "I have sold four of the knives."

"Try something small, for they won't want to carry bulky packages with them. I see there are a lot of young fellows drifting in. You might get out the mouth harmonicas and interest them in them. I'll show those ladies the jewelry, and try to make some more private sales."

To this Matt agreed, and he was soon playing a lively air that caused all of the young men and boys to gather around him.

"Any one can play if he has music in him and such an instrument as this in his possession," he argued, after he had finished. " To show that it is all right and in perfect tune, I will put up the one I have been playing upon. How much am I offered?"

" Ten cents!" cried a boy standing close at hand.

" Ten cents I am offered. Ten ce——"

Matt got no further, for at that moment a loud' cry upon the street drowned out every other sound

" Look out for the bear! He is mad!"

" He is coming this way!"

" Scatter for your lives!"

These and a hundred other cries rent the air. Then came a crash of window glass, and the next moment a huge brown bear leaped into the show window, not over two yards away from where Matt was standing.

CHAPTER XV.

THE CHARMS OF MUSIC.

For the moment after the brown bear crashed through the glass and landed in the show window of the auction store Matt was too astonished to move.

The entrance of the great beast, which had undoubtedly escaped from the circus men during the parade, was so totally unexpected that all in the place were too paralyzed with fear to move.

Screams of terror rent the air, and to these the brown bear added a growl which was both deep and angry.

Andy, who stood some distance behind Matt, was the first to do any rational talking.

"Grab the pistol, Matt!" he exclaimed. "Grab it quick!"

The weapon to which Andy referred was lying under the counter, just in front of the boy. It had been purchased by the firm and placed there in case some ugly person raised a dispute, or a sneak-thief tried to run off with any article. Andy had said that the mere sight of a pistol would often bring matters to terms when words had no effect.

Matt understood his partner's cry, and he lost no time in acting upon it. He caught up the pistol, and at once aimed it at the bear's head.

Whether or not the beast understood that his life was in danger would be hard to say, but no sooner had the weapon been pointed at him than he arose on his hind legs and emitted a growl that was fairly blood-curdling to the involuntary listeners.

Matt did not claim to be a crack shot, having had but slight experience in pistol practice, and, even in that moment of peril, he hesitated to shoot, fearful of missing the bear and striking some one on the sidewalk outside.

"Clear the way out there!" he cried. "Clear the way, or you may get shot!"

His words had the effect of scattering the few venturesome persons who had collected to see what the bear might do. In the meantime those in the store ran out of the open doors as quickly as they could. Andy alone remained with his partner, arming himself with the longest carving-knife the stock afforded.

Once on his hind legs the brown bear hesitated in his movements. He was separated from Matt by five feet of space between the show window and the raised platform upon which the boy stood. He did not seem to wish to leap the span, nor did he appear inclined to step down to the floor and then up upon the platform.

"Why don't you let him have it?" yelled Andy, as he saw Matt raise the pistol and then lower it again.

"I don't believe he's so mad after all," returned the boy. "I'm not going to shoot until I have to. Say!" he went on suddenly, "give him a tune on one of the accordions."

"What's that?" gasped Andy in astonishment.

"Play him a tune. He may be a trained bear, and if so, the music may soothe him."

Andy at once caught Matt's idea, and, taking up an accordion which stood close at hand, he began a lively tune of a popular sort.

At the first bars of the tune the brown bear appeared surprised. He raised himself up higher than ever on his hind legs, until his head touched the top of the show window. Then he started as if to dance, crashing over every article which was on exhibition. Finding he could not dance in the limited space around him, he leaped to the pavement outside, and there, to the bystanders' amazement and relief, began to execute a clumsy jig.

"He's dancing, sure enough!" cried Andy. "That was a good idea of yours, Matt."

"Keep it up until his keepers come," returned the boy. "Lively, now, Andy, for playing means something."

Andy continued to play, and as the brown bear began to dance more heartily than ever, the people, who a moment before had been so frightened, gathered about and began to laugh.

"That's better than shooting him," remarked one man.

"Indeed, it is," returned another. "Keep it up, young fellow!"

And Andy did keep it up until two keepers appeared, hatless and almost out of breath, and took the bear in charge.

"Doxie would have been all right," one of them explained; "but while he was performing on the square below some mischievous boy threw some pepper in his mouth."

"Yes, and Doxie went after him," added the other. "It's lucky for the boy that he got out of sight, for had Doxie caught him he would have chewed him up."

"I am very thankful that he did not do any further damage," said Matt. "I thought I would have to shoot him," and he exhibited the pistol.

"It's lucky for you that you didn't shoot Doxie," cried the head keeper. "You would have been a couple of hundred out of pocket."

"That reminds me," put in Andy. "Who is going to pay for that smashed show window and the ruined goods?"

At this the faces of the two keepers fell. The brown bear had been in their keeping, and they knew that the proprietor of the circus would hold them responsible for any damage done.

"Well, that is not our fault," returned the head keeper blandly. "I reckon you will have to bear the loss yourselves."

"Indeed, not!" cried Matt. "The owner of this bear will pay every cent."

"Well, go on and see him, then," returned the keeper curtly, and throwing a chain over the bear's head, he started to lead the animal away.

"Hold on," said Andy quietly but firmly. "You will not take that bear away until this matter is settled. Matt, see if you can find a policeman."

A policeman was close at hand, and he was at once summoned. A long altercation followed, in which the keepers tried to disown any responsibility in the matter.

"Whom does the bear belong to?" questioned Andy at last.

"Mr. Menville, the proprietor of the show."

"Then you leave him here until Mr. Menville comes for him," was the quick reply. "Mr. Officer, please see to it that the bear is not taken away. I think he might very easily be chained to that hitching-post by the curb."

"Sure, an' Oi dunno about this!" exclaimed the policeman, an old Irishman. "Ye had better let him take the baste away."

"No, he'll stay here until damages are settled," said Andy. "They do not own the bear, and if they attempt to take him away arrest them both."

Andy did not know if he was acting according to law or not, and, for that matter, neither did the policeman. But the auctioneer's firm stand had the desired effect, for the two keepers presently weakened, and asked what it would cost to replace the window and the goods spoiled.

A glazier was called in, and while he was figuring Matt and Andy went over the stock. At the end of ten minutes it was found that sixteen dollars would cover all loss. With much grumbling the circus men paid the amount, and they were then permitted to lead the brown bear away.

"Quite a bit of excitement, I must say," was Matt's comment after it was all over. "I don't want to go through any such scare again."

"Nor I," returned Andy. "But, see, there is quite a crowd gathered around yet. Let us make the most of the chance."

"I am too unstrung to auction off any stuff," admitted Matt. "That first scare was enough to take the heart right out of a fellow. You go ahead if you wish, and I'll clean out the window and get things ready for that new frame and glass."

So without further delay Andy began to address the people, and soon he had the store once more filled. He kept on auctioning stuff off until one o'clock in the afternoon, when the crowd thinned out, being composed principally of folks who had come into the city to visit the circus.

By that time Matt had set the carpenter and the glazier to work, and the new woodwork and the glass were in. All it needed was a couple of coats of paint, and the show window would be as good as new. The owner of the building, having heard of the affair, came around to view the situation, and expressed himself perfectly satisfied with what had been done.

"And I'm glad you made them pay up on the spot," he said. "For if those circus people had been allowed to leave town I would never have gotten a cent."

And to show his gratitude, he bought a razor and

strop for himself, and a pair of scissors for his wife.

"There will not be much doing now until evening," said Andy to Matt. "So we will have dinner and then one of us can deliver those articles that lady bought."

"I'll deliver the stuff, Andy. I fancy the walk will brace me up more than anything else would."

"Well, go on then," said Andy, and so, after he had had dinner, Matt set out with the bundle of goods under his arm.

The way to the lady's house led past the circus. and with a natural curiosity to see what was going on, Matt pushed his way through the crowd to where a number of banners were stretched containing vivid pictures of the many wonderful sights which the ticket seller said could be seen within.

The boy was much interested in the slick way of speaking which the ticket seller had, and to "gain points," as he called it, for the auction business, he remained almost an hour listening to all that was said.

He was about to leave the crowd when a well-dressed man who was standing beside him pushed him a bit to one side, and then stooped to pick something from the ground at Matt's feet.

It was a large pocket-book, and apparently well filled.

CHAPTER XVI.

THE CONFIDENCE MAN.

" By Jove ! look at that !" cried the man, in a low tone, as he picked up the pocket-book and surveyed it. " That's a find, isn't it?"

" It is, indeed," returned Matt. " How much is there in it ?"

" Come with me and I'll see," said the man, and without waiting for Matt to offer a reply, he caught the boy by the arm, and forced him through the crowd to an open spot behind a large tree.

" I would like to know who lost this," went on the man, as he opened the flap of the pocket-book, and gazed inside at the contents. " By Jove ! look at that pile of bills !" he went on, as he turned the pocket-book around so that Matt might catch sight of what certainly did look like twenty-five or thirty bank bills tucked away in one of the pockets. " Must be a hundred dollars or more in it."

" The owner of that pocket-book will miss it,"

returned Matt. "You ought to make an effort to find him."

"Of course! of course!" assented the man heartily. "I don't want to keep anybody's money—not if I know it is theirs. Let me see if there is a card in it."

He turned the pocket-book around and put his fingers first in one pocket and then another.

"Not a blessed thing but that pile of bills," he went on. "Now, isn't that strange?"

Then he suddenly drew from his vest pocket a gold watch and looked at it.

"Quarter to three!" he exclaimed in a startled tone. "And I must catch the three o'clock train for Baltimore! I haven't time to look up the owner of this pocket-book, valuable as it is."

"You might take a later train," suggested Matt.

The man shook his head.

"No, I have an engagement in Baltimore immediately upon the arrival of this train which I would not miss for a dozen such pocket-books."

"Then you'll have to take the money with you."

"I wouldn't feel just right about doing that," returned the man with a bland smile. "I would feel like a thief. I'll tell you what I will do," he went on smoothly and earnestly. "Give me twenty dollars, and you take the pocket-book. Perhaps you won't be able to find an owner, and then the money will all be yours, and if you do find an owner, he will certainly offer more of a reward than twenty dollars."

" I take the pocket-book?" said Matt, considerably surprised by the offer.

" Yes; I really can't wait, and I do not feel satisfied to take that money with me."

" But, supposing I do not find the owner, do you not want part of the money?"

" No; you can keep it all."

This certainly seemed a very liberal offer, and had Matt had less experience of the world at large, he might have accepted on the spot. But the apparent open-heartedness of the stranger only served to make him more cautious.

" Let us count the money and see how much there is in the pocket-book," he remarked, hardly knowing what else to say.

" No, I haven't time to do that," said the stranger hastily. " As it is, I have now barely ten minutes in which to get to the depot. If you want to accept my offer, give me the twenty dollars, and I'll run for the depot."

And the man moved around as if in the greatest hurry of his life.

"I haven't twenty dollars with me."

" Indeed! I thought you looked like a well-to-do young man——"

" I have twelve dollars——"

" Well—let that do, but be quick!"

And the stranger held out his hand for the amount.

" Never mind," remarked Matt, struck with an idea which he resolved to carry out if he went into the scheme at all. " I'll take the money from the pocket-book, and if I find the owner I will tell him how I came to do it."

" No ; don't you touch the contents of the pocket-book!" exclaimed the stranger, hastily snatching the article in question from Matt's hand. " That would not be right!"

" Yes, but I will make it right with the owner, if I——"

" I can't wait any longer for that train!" cried the stranger, and without another word he placed the pocket-book into his coat-pocket and disappeared into the crowd.

For the instant Matt stared after him, and then a light burst upon the boy's mind.

" He is a confidence man and was trying to swindle me!" he murmured to himself. " If that pocket-book contained much it was a single dollar bill on a pile of green paper! How lucky I was not to jump at his offer when he first made it!"

As soon as he had reached this conclusion, Matt made after the man. But the crowd was too thick and too large to find him, and after a quarter of an hour's search the young auctioneer gave it up.

It was now getting late, and as soon as he was satisfied that the confidence man was gone, Matt hurried along on his errand.

He found that the lady who had purchased the goods had just reached home. She had heard of the brown bear episode, and insisted upon Matt giving her the particulars, which he did. She was very much interested in his story, and after she had heard how the affair terminated she plied him with questions concerning the auction business.

"You may think me very curious," she said at length. "But the reason I ask is because my only son, Tom Inwold, ran away with a traveling auctioneer about three months ago."

"Ran away?" repeated Matt.

"Yes ; he got into a difficulty in school, and when I insisted that he apologize to his teachers, he grew angry and left the house."

"How old was he?"

"Tom was fifteen last May."

"He was very young to become an auctioneer,"

smiled Matt. "I am hardly old enough for the business."

"He has made a friend of this auctioneer—who used to stand up in a wagon and sing songs, and then sell cheap jewelry—and he went off with him one Saturday, when I thought he had gone to New York with his uncle."

"And doesn't he want to come back?" asked Matt, deeply interested.

"I have never heard of him since he went away." Mrs. Inwold put her handkerchief to her eyes to dry the tears which had started. "One reason I wished these goods delivered was because I thought I might get a chance to talk to you about Tom. You intend to travel from place to place, do you not?"

"Yes, madam; we shall remain here but a few days."

"Then, perhaps, in your travels you may run across Tom. If you do I wish you would tell him to send word home. He ought to come home of himself, but I suppose he won't do that, he is so headstrong."

"I should think he would prefer a good home to traveling around with a cheap jewelry man," was Matt's comment, as he looked around at the comfortable house Mrs. Inwold occupied. "I know I would."

"Boys do not always know what is best for them," sighed the lady. "Tom generally had his own way, and that made him headstrong. He is my only son, and as his father is away most of the time, I suppose I treated him more indulgently than was good for him."

"You have no idea where he and the jewelry man went?"

"Not the slightest. I notified the police and sent out several detectives, but could learn nothing. The detectives told me that the jewelry man was little better than a thief, and always covered his tracks when he left a city, so that his victims could not trace him up."

"That's most likely true. But I trust you do not take my partner and me for such fellows," added Matt honestly.

"No; you look like a young gentleman, and the other young man was one, too, I feel sure."

"We try to do things on the square. We never willfully misrepresent what we sell—as many do."

"That is right, and if you keep on that way you will be bound to prosper. No one ever yet gained much by resorting to trickery in trying to get along."

Mrs. Inwold talked to Matt for quite awhile after this, and promised to come down to the store and buy several other articles of which she thought she stood in need. It was nearly five o'clock when the boy left the mansion.

"A very nice lady," thought Matt, as he hurried back to the auction store. "I hope I meet her son Tom some day. I'll tell him how she feels about his going away, and advise him to return home without delay. My gracious! you wouldn't catch me leaving a home like that in order to put up with the hardships of the road!"

CHAPTER XVII.

THE STORM.

That evening Matt and Andy were kept busy until nearly eleven o'clock selling goods to people that came from the circus. They put up nearly every kind of article on their shelves, and only about half the stock remained unsold when they finally closed and locked the doors.

"That circus was a windfall to us!" exclaimed Andy. "We would not have done half as well had it not been in town."

"Maybe it would be a good idea to follow up the circus," suggested Matt. "That seems to draw out the people more than anything else I know of."

"We will follow the circus as much as we can, Matt. But there is one thing I must do first."

"And what is that?"

"Take the first train back to New York in the morning and buy more goods. Some of our best sellers are entirely gone."

"Then go by all means," returned Matt quickly.

" But can you get along alone ?"

" I guess so. If I can't I'll lock up till you get back."

"All right, then. Now let us go over the stock and I'll make out a list of what's wanted."

" Let us figure up what we have made," returned Matt quickly, for he was anxious to know what the exact amount would be.

" Very well; I would like to know myself."

On a sheet of paper they had kept a record of every article sold, with the price. Opposite these, Andy, who was more familiar with their cost than Matt, placed the amount of profit on each. Then with his partner leaning over his shoulder, he added the column up.

"Thirty-one dollars and a quarter!" exclaimed Matt, as he surveyed the result of Andy's calculations. " Did we really make as much as that ?"

" We did. Of course we must take out our personal expenses and Billy's keep. That amounts to four dollars and a quarter nearly."

" That still leaves twenty-seven dollars for one day's work. At this rate we'll get rich fast."

" We must not expect such luck every day, Matt. Remember, to-day was circus day. We will have rainy days, and days spent in traveling, during which we will not take in anything, while our expenses go on just the same."

"But it's a good thing we didn't have that kind of a start, Andy. We would have been 'busted' otherwise."

"You are right there," returned Andy.

By seven o'clock on the following morning he was on the way to New York, leaving Matt to open the store alone. This the young auctioneer did, and as trade was very quiet, Matt spent the time in cleaning up such goods as had been handled, and tidying up generally.

Compared with the day before, the street was almost deserted, but during the noon hour, when people were going to and coming from dinner, Matt managed to start up a sale which lasted until nearly two o'clock, and by which he disposed of over three dollars' worth of goods at a good profit.

It was nearly seven o'clock when Andy returned. He had rushed matters in New York, but had bought several bargains, especially one in imitation cut glassware, which, when it arrived the next day, made a pretty showing in the window.

They remained in Plainfield two days longer, and then loaded their wagon once more and started on the road. They made brief stops at Bound Brook and Somerville, doing fairly well at both places, and then, just ten days after leaving the city, struck Flemington.

At this latter place they again came across Menville's circus, and as a consequence did a big day's business. They intended to leave Flemington on the day following, but after talking the matter over decided to remain until the following Monday.

" On Monday morning you can strike across the country for High Bridge alone, if you will," said Andy. " I can take another trip to New York, and buy more goods and have them shipped direct to that place, or else on to Phillipsburg, which shall be our last stopping place in New Jersey."

To this Matt agreed, and on Saturday night all was made ready for an early morning start on Monday. Sunday was a quiet day for both, although they attended divine services, and took a long walk among the farms outside of the town proper.

" By creation! but it looks like a storm," exclaimed Andy, on Monday morning, as he jumped out of bed and aroused Matt.

" Well, if it rains we will have to make the most of it, I suppose," returned the boy philosophically " It's a pity we haven't any umbrellas to sell !"

" There! I'll put them on the list at once !" cried Andy, with a laugh. " I declare, Matt, you are getting to be more of a business man every day."

" If I am it's because I have such a good partner
for a teacher, Andy."

" Oh, nonsense," returned the young man, but
nevertheless considerably pleased to learn that Matt
appreciated his efforts. " You are as bright as any
one on the road."

When they went down to the dining-room of the
hotel at which they were stopping it certainly did
look like rain. Yet there was a brisk breeze blowing, and several expressed themselves as certain that
it would pass around to the north of them.

Less than half an hour later Andy was on his way
to the depot to catch a train, and Matt hurried to
the stable where Billy and the wagon were.

" I'll get to High Bridge just as soon as I can,"
he said to himself. " I have no desire to be caught
in a thunder-storm on a strange country road."

" You may get a bit wet, but that's all," remarked
the stable-keeper, as he saw the boy glance at the
heavy clouds scurrying across the sky. " That there
storm, if it comes, which is doubtful, won't last half
an hour."

With this reassurance, if such it could be called,
Matt saw to it that all was in good condition, and
sprang upon the seat. He had made careful inquiries concerning the road, so that he might not go
astray—a thing easy to do in most parts of the

country—and in a short space of time he was out of the town and on the turnpike.

Had it been a pleasant day the boy would have enjoyed that drive thoroughly, for it was through a most beautiful section of the country. On both sides of the road were broad fields, dotted here and there with patches of woods and bushes. Several brooks were also crossed, and at one of these he stopped for a few minutes to watch a trio of boys fishing.

But then the sky seemed to grow darker suddenly, and somewhat alarmed, Matt whipped up Billy. The wind died out utterly, and the air grew close and sultry.

"That means a heavy thunder-storm and nothing less," thought Matt. "I wish I was near the journey's end instead of only about half through with it."

Presently came a sudden and quite unexpected rush of wind, and a second later a heavy dash of rain, which drove almost into the boy's face.

Matt at once stopped driving, and adjusted the rubber blanket in front of his seat. This was no easy job, for the wind kept increasing in violence. He had barely completed the work when there came a crash of thunder, and then the rain came down harder than ever.

"I wish I could find some shelter," he muttered to himself. " I would willingly pay to be allowed to drive into some barn until this was over. I hope none of the stock gets wet."

Matt tried to peer about him, but he could not see far, owing to the sheets of rain which fell all around.

" We'll have to stick to the road until something comes in sight, Billy," he said, addressing the shivering horse. " Get up old boy, and step lively."

Thus addressed, the animal started on once more. But the rain prevented him going as fast as before. The ground was very heavy, and the road in spots was covered with water which had not time to run off, so heavy was the downpour.

Presently they came to where the road ran through a heavy bit of timber. Here it was almost as dark as night, and the branches of the trees, laden with water, hung down so low that many swept the wagon as the turn-out went by.

" Ugh! I wish we were out of this!" muttered Matt, as he tried in vain to pierce the gloom ahead. " You must find the road, Billy, for I can't see it——"

A terrific crash of thunder drowned out the last words. Billy sprang forward in alarm, and away

.

A PERILOUS DRIVE

went the wagon over rocks and decaying tree trunks.

"Whoa!" shouted Matt. "Whoa, Billy, whoa! You have left the road, old boy! Whoa!"

But now a blinding flash of lightning lit up the scene, and then came another crash of thunder, even louder than before. Billy reared up, and then came down with a leap. On the instant he was off, like a rocket, over bushes, logs and rocks, dragging the swaying and creaking wagon after him!

CHAPTER XVIII.

A "HOLD-UP."

For the time being, Matt, on the seat of the heavily-laden wagon, felt certain that the entire turn-out must come to grief, and that very soon. Billy, thoroughly frightened by the thunder and lightning, was straining every nerve to make his way through the woods, despite brush, stones, and fallen trees.

Between the flashes of light the way beneath the trees was almost totally dark. The rain swept this way and that, and Matt, standing up on the foot-rest, was soaked to the skin.

" Whoa, Billy, old boy! Whoa!" he called again. " You are all right!"

But the scared horse paid no attention to his call. His nerves seemed to be strained to their utmost, and on he plunged, dragging the wagon along with bumps and jolts, which more than once threatened to land the young auctioneer out on his head.

Realizing that something must be done quickly if

he would save the wagon from becoming a total wreck, Matt resolved upon a bold move. He tied the reins to the dashboard, and then, with a swift jump, cast himself upon Billy's back.

For the instant the horse, worse frightened than before, tore along over the uneven surface at a greater rate of speed than ever. The wagon struck a rock, and seemed about to lurch over upon its side. But it righted, and seeing this, Matt began to talk to the horse, patting him in the meanwhile upon the neck in an affectionate way.

This show of kindness soon had more effect upon Billy than anything which had previously been done. The animal slackened his speed gradually, and then, as there came a brief lull in the storm, stopped short, almost winded, but still inclined to go on at the first sign of further danger.

As soon as Billy had come to a halt Matt sprang to the ground. A tree the boy had feared they would collide with was close at hand, and to this he tied the horse, making sure that the halter should be well secured; and for the time being, the danger of being wrecked through a runaway was over.

But the trouble was by no means past. The storm still kept on, the lightning being as vivid as ever, and the thunder causing Billy to tug violently at the strap which held him. It was with a shiver that Matt wondered what the consequence would be should that particular tree be struck by lightning.

To prevent Billy doing damage to the wagon by twisting in the shafts or by kicking, Matt unharnessed him and pushed the wagon back a few feet into a somewhat open space. Here the rain came down heavier, but he felt safer than in close proximity to the tree.

Feeling that nothing was to be done until the storm should abate, Matt climbed into the wagon again and protected himself as well as he coul l with the rubber blanket and the lap-robe. The back shade of the wagon was down, and he was glad to see that so far the stock inside had sustained no damage.

A half-hour dragged along slowly. Several times the storm appeared upon the point of clearing away, but each time the clouds settled down heavier than before, until under the trees it was as black as midnight.

Matt wondered how far he was from the road, and if there were a farmhouse anywhere at hand.

" If I could reach a house of some sort it wouldn't be so bad," he murmured to himself. "But being out here alone isn't any fun, that's certain."

At last the clouds seemed to scatter for good. A fresh breeze stirred the trees and bushes, and ere

long the rain ceased, although the drops still came
down from the heavily-laden branches overhead.

As soon as he felt certain that the sky was brightening to remain so, Matt untied Billy, and harnessed
him to the wagon once more.

"Now, Billy, we'll get back to the road just as
fast as we can," he said to the horse. "And I trust
that you will never run away again in that fashion,
old boy."

On all sides arose bushes and rocks, and, although
the road might be close at hand, Matt thought it
best to return the way they had come. He wished
to take no more chances, feeling that it would be
the easiest thing in the world to get lost, or to run
the turn-out into some hollow or hole from which
it would be next to impossible to extricate it.

But to return by the route they had come was
itself no easy task. In his terror, Billy had dragged
the heavy vehicle over several very uneven places,
full of stumps and rocks, and now the animal, still
somewhat exhausted, had all he could do to move
back over the trail which had been left.

Matt led the horse, and on more than one occasion had to place his shoulder to the rear end of the
wagon to help over a particularly bad spot. Thus
they moved on, taking half an hour to cover a dis-

tance which had previously been traveled in less than half that time.

"Thank goodness, we are out of that at last!" exclaimed Matt, as the road finally appeared in sight. "Now to see if any damage has been done."

The young auctioneer made a minute examination of every bolt and spring, as well as of the running gear and harness. He was overjoyed to find everything still in good order, despite the rough usage to which it had been put. The wagon body was scratched in a dozen places, but this could be easily remedied.

The rubber blankets were put away, and the laprobe left fluttering in the rear to dry, and then Matt once more resumed his lonely journey in the direction of High Bridge.

The heavy rain had left the road deep with mud, and through this Billy plodded slowly along, Matt not having the heart to urge him to a greater speed, knowing well that the faithful animal was doing as well as could be reasonably expected of him.

"As soon as we reach High Bridge I must find a good stable for Billy, and change my clothes," thought Matt. "And something hot to drink won't go bad, either. Ugh! I am chilled clear to the bone!"

And he gave a shiver that was as genuine as it was uncomfortable.

The road now led downward and around a bend, where was situated another heavy bit of timber. As Matt approached the wood he saw some distance back from the road a shanty built of rough logs and boards, and thatched with weather-beaten shingles and bits of old tin and oil-cloth. There was a rude chimney upon the outside of the rear of this shanty, and from this a thin cloud of smoke was issuing.

"Humph! here is somebody's home, but a very poor one," thought Matt. "I shouldn't wonder but those inside got a pretty good soaking, by the looks of things."

At first the young auctioneer determined to stop, but upon second thought, he concluded to go on, satisfied that no accommodations worthy of the name could be had there.

"If I can't strike something better, I'll keep right on to High Bridge," was his thought, and he was just about to urge Billy on once more, when the door of the shanty opened and a man came out.

The man was apparently fifty years of age, and rough in looks. His beard was long, as was also his hair, and both seemed to be much in need of shears and brush. His clothing and his face were dirty, and altogether he presented a decidedly ill-favored appearance.

"Hullo, there, stranger!" he called out. "Where bound?"

"Bound for High Bridge," replied Matt as he drew rein. "How many miles is it?"

"Not many," was the rather indefinite reply. "Suppose you got cotched in that storm, eh?"

"Yes, I got the full benefit of it."

"It was a heavy one, no mistake about that. What sort of a turn-out have you got there?"

"An auction goods wagon."

"Carrying stuff around the country to sell at auction?"

"Yes."

"I see. Say, maybe you've got something you would like to sell me," and the man, after speaking to some one in the shanty, stepped up closer to the turn-out.

"Perhaps I have, but it's pretty well packed up," returned Matt, who was not at all taken by the man's manner. "We'll be open at High Bridge this evening, or to-morrow, if nothing happens."

"We? Got somebody else with you?"

"Not on the wagon, but I have a partner."

"I see. What line of goods do you carry?"

Matt named over a number of articles. The man's eyes brightened as he listened.

"Let me have a pair of suspenders," he said. "I need them worst way. And if you've got a good pocket-knife I'll patronize you so much more. Drive up in the back of the house and tie fast anywhere."

"Excuse me, but I would prefer getting to High Bridge. I am wet to the skin, and I want to change my clothes."

"That's all right, young fellow. We've got a fire inside, and you can dry yourself there just as well as not."

"But my horse——"

"I'll take care of the horse. I've got a shed a bit back of those bushes. Come on in; what are you afraid of?"

Thus urged, Matt sprang from the wagon seat to the ground. As he did so he noted a look of satisfaction gleam upon the man's dirty face, and he saw the fellow wave his hand toward the shanty's one window. He turned swiftly in the direction, and was in time to see two equally repulsive heads dodge aside out of sight.

Only for a second did the young auctioneer hesitate. Then something warned him to beware of danger, and he turned again to the wagon and placed one foot upon the shaft step.

"Hi! what are you going to do?" cried the man, in surprise.

"I guess I won't stop," returned the boy. "That storm does not seem to be quite over, and I do not wish to catch a second dose."

"But you will stop, sonny!" exclaimed the man, with a sudden change of manner. "Hi, Jake! Baldy! Come out here and help me manage this young fellow!" he went on, in a louder tone.

The other men at once rushed from the shanty, and in a trice Matt was surrounded.

CHAPTER XIX.

OUT OF A BAD SCRAPE.

It did not take the young auctioneer long to understand the true nature of the situation in which he now found himself. The three men who had surrounded him were nothing more or less than tramps who had undoubtedly sought shelter in the shanty from the storm. That they were thoroughly unscrupulous men went without saying, and it must be confessed that Matt's heart sank within him as he realized the danger in which he was placed.

"Let go of me!" he said sternly to the first man, who had presumed to catch him by the arm. "Let go, I say!"

"Don't you do it, Crabs!" put in the tramp called Jake. "Hold tight to him while I tie up the hoss."

"What do you mean to do?" demanded Matt, as he struggled to free himself, but in vain.

"You'll learn fast enough, sonny," returned Crabs, with a wicked grin. "Just keep quiet now, will you?"

"I certainly shall not!" retorted the young auctioneer hotly. "Do you suppose I am going to submit tamely to being robbed?"

"Who said anything about robbin' you?" demanded the third tramp, he called Baldy, although his head was covered with a shock of hair twice as thick as either of his companions. "You had better act civil-like, sonny, if you want to get off without a licking."

"You let me go!" went on Matt, paying no attention to the last remark. "Let go, I say—or take the consequences!"

"The consequences?" sneered him called Crabs.

"Yes—there!"

And without further warning, Matt drew back with his clinched fist and gave the tramp a stinging blow between the eyes, which caused the much surprised individual to let go his hold and stagger back to the shanty's side.

"Ho—what—what do you mean by hitting me?" he howled.

"I told you to let go," retorted Matt; and free from his tormentor, he essayed to leap to the wagon seat and gain possession of the heavy whip, with which he might keep the tramps at bay.

But hardly had he placed his foot on the rest than Baldy, who was now close at hand, caught him by

the ankle and gave a sudden jerk, which brought
Matt down on his chest and face, scratching his left
cheek in two places, and giving him a severe shaking
up.

"Hold the horse, Jake!" cried Baldy. "Hold the
horse, and I'll hold the boy."

"Let me get at him!" cried Crabs, in a rage.
"Just let me get at him, and I'll teach him to strike
me between the eyes!"

As he spoke he rushed past his companion, and
was on the point of kicking Matt in the side when
Baldy stopped him with a side dig of his ragged
elbow.

"Don't strike him if it ain't necessary," he said.
"I'll hold him all right enough. Come, be still
now," he went on to the young auctioneer.

Matt was on his face on the ground and Baldy
was sitting on top of him, but, nevertheless, the boy
did not intend to give up the struggle.

He squirmed and twisted this way and that until
finally free, and then, before the tramp could catch
him again, he sprang to his feet and leaped upon
the foot-rest of the wagon.

"Stand back there, all of you!" he cried determinedly, and the next instant had the whip and was
flourishing it over the heads of those below him.

"See that! he's got away from you!" cried Crabs

to Baldy, in tones of deep disgust. "Now don't
you wish you had let me tend to him?"

"Stick to the horse, Jake!" cried Baldy, ignoring
the last remark. "I'll soon have the young fellow
on the ground again."

"Let go of that horse!" commanded Matt. "Let
go, or I'll lash you right and left!"

The tramp called Jake looked up into the young
auctioneer's face at these words. Evidently he did
not like the looks of the set lines about Matt's
mouth, for without delay he obeyed the order, and
stepped back. He had hardly done so before Matt
struck Billy a light blow, and off went the horse at
quite a respectable gait, leaving the three would-be
plunderers standing staring after the turn-out in
wonder and disgust!

"Phew! but that was a narrow escape!" gasped
Matt, to himself, as he caught up the lines and gave
Billy another tap. "I suppose I ought to be thankful that I was not robbed of everything in my
keeping. Those fellows looked wicked enough to
do almost anything."

After he had gone on some little distance he
leaned out of the wagon to see if he was being pur-
sued. But the tramps had deemed it unwise to
follow him, and once more the young auctioneer
had the road to himself.

It was not long before the houses of High Bridge
appeared in sight. At the first place the young
auctioneer asked for directions to the hotel, and
here he had the wagon and horse safely stabled,
and then went to the room which had been assigned to him to change every article of clothing
he wore.

He had ordered a hot meal to be served, and
when he came down he found the table spread for
him.

"Got caught in the shower, eh?" questioned the
hotel-keeper, as Matt sat down.

"Yes, indeed," returned the boy, and he related
the particulars of his adventures while eating, not
forgetting to mention the three tramps.

"Those three rascals have been bothering folks
around here for quite a bit," remarked the hotel-
keeper after he had finished. "The constable is
after 'em now, but I don't think he'll catch 'em, for
they slide around from place to place. You can bet
on it that they are miles away from that shanty by
this time."

"Well, I trust that I never fall in with them
again," returned Matt with a slight shudder.

"Going to hold an auction?" went on the hotel-
keeper curiously.

"That's what I expect to do. I would like to find

some good spot. Where would be the best place
for me to locate, do you think?"

The hotel-keeper thought for a moment.

"Well, most of the folks come around here and
over across the way to the general stores. But
I reckon the store-keepers won't like you around
much."

"They never do—but I can't help that. I've got
to make a living as well as they."

"That's true. Tell you what you might do.
There's the old paint-shop next door. You can use
that for an auction place if you are a mind to be
liberal for the use of it," said the hotel-keeper.

As soon as he had finished Matt went out and in-
spected the old paint-shop. He found it would do
very well for his purpose, and on returning offered
the hotel-keeper a good pocket-knife for its use for
the following day. This offer was at once accepted,
and Matt set to work without delay to get the place
into shape.

By nightfall he was ready for business. In the
meantime, he had sent a couple of small boys
around to all the houses in the neighborhood to
notify the folks of the sale, and as a consequence,
by eight o'clock he had the shop quite comfortably
filled.

Without waiting to see if Andy might return on

the late evening train, Matt started up business, and inside of half an hour had matters in full swing. He opened up with a lot of goods which the folks appeared to need, and they sold readily, much to the disgust of one of the proprietors of the regular stores, who came over to see what was going on.

"Humph! it's only a boy!" he muttered, but loud enough for all to hear. "What does he know about the goods he is selling? Like as not they are second-handed, and all shop-worn."

"These goods are strictly new, and of the latest designs," called out Matt, looking squarely at the man. "They are direct from New York, and I venture to say cannot be duplicated in High Bridge at the price at which I am knocking them down for. Now, ladies and gentlemen, what am I offered for this elegant family album, bound in plush, with sliver-plated clasps?"

"One dollar!" called a rustic, standing close at hand.

"A dollar and a quarter!" shouted a farmer near the door.

"See here, Podders, you ought to buy your things of me," whispered the keeper of the general store to the latter bidder. "I trust you till the money for crops comes in."

"So you do—and I pay you for the accommodation, too," retorted the farmer.

"I can sell you an album for half the money he'll charge you."

"I don't know about that," returned the farmer, with a shake of his head.

"Yes, I can. Come on over to the store and see."

"I want to watch this sale first."

By this time another person had offered a dollar and a half for the album, and Matt was hard at work trying to get a raise on this figure. But he overheard the store-keeper's words, and his face flushed with indignation. He stopped short, and pointed directly at the man.

"Will you please come forward a moment?" he asked, in a loud and clear tone.

"What—what's that?" stammered the store-keeper, taken by surprise.

"I asked you if you would please come forward."

"What for?"

"I wish to ask you what right you have to come in here and endeavor to take away my possible customers?"

"Why, you—I ain't taken any one away."

"But you were just trying to induce that man to leave—told him you could sell him an album for half the money I would charge."

"What if I did—I can, too."

"I doubt it. If you could, folks would not flock to such an auction-sale as this. They come here because they can get things cheap—because they are not overcharged, as they are in some places—because they are told the truth about goods—because they like to see a boy get along in spite of what some mean man may do to take away his business —because they——"

But Matt could go no further. His unexpected speech brought forth a sudden applause that for the moment drowned out every other sound.

CHAPTER XX.

ACCUSED OF STEALING.

It was plain to see that the store-keeper who had thus thrust himself into the young auctioneer's business was not in high favor with the residents of the country town. To tell the truth, the man was not liked by any one, and was only patronized by force of circumstances or through long-standing habit. He was a thoroughly mean man, and the fact that his trade had been falling off steadily for several years had not tended to sweeten his temper.

" That's one on Ike Marvelling, sure!" laughed a young man near the auction stand.

" Yes, an' Ike deserves it," returned a woman beside him. " He has no right to come in here and abuse the boy."

" That's so, he ain't," added another woman.

" Ike was always high-priced in everything," remarked a jolly-faced farmer. "If he had Pickle Mountain to sell he would want double price for it."

This bit of humor caused a laugh at the store-keeper's expense, and put him in even worse humor than had Matt's caustic remarks.

"See here, I didn't come in here to be abused!" he cried, addressing the young auctioneer in a bullying tone.

"You were not asked in here at all, to my knowl edge," returned Matt. "And you should have remained away unless you intended to do the right thing."

"See here, boy, what do you mean?"

"What would you think of me if I came over to your store and told your customers that I could sell them goods cheaper than you could? I rather guess you would be for running me out—and mighty lively, too!"

"That he would!" laughed several. "He wouldn't give you time to open your mouth."

"I came in here because I know all these auction sales—they ain't really auctions at all—are frauds!" blustered Isaac Marvelling, finding it hard to say anything in the face of so much opposition. "These chaps oughten to be allowed to sell a thing—they swindle folks so, and if I had my way, the constable would——"

"Stop right there!" interrupted Matt, his eyes flashing. "When you insinuate that I am a swindler, you go too far. You must take back those words!"

"Must I?" sneered the store-keeper. "Well, I reckon not."

"Very well, then." Matt turned to several men standing by the door. "Will one of you gentlemen kindly call in the constable or some other officer?"

"What—what do you mean?" asked Isaac Marvelling in a lower tone, and much disturbed.

"I mean to have you put out as a disorderly character, that's what I mean," returned Matt firmly. "I have paid my license, and so long as I do business on the square I do not intend to allow any one to bulldoze me or call me a swindler."

"That's right! That's right!" cried several men in the crowd, and the woman who had first spoken nodded approvingly.

"You're a mighty big boy!" sneered the store-keeper, but all noticed that he retreated several steps toward the open doorway.

"I am big enough to defend myself," replied the young auctioneer quickly. "I want you to leave. I am no more of a swindler than you are—perhaps not as much. I am conducting this business on an honest basis, and I will not stand by and let you or any one else blacken my character."

"We'll see—we'll see," muttered Isaac Marvel-

ling, and greatly enraged, but unable to say a word
in his own defense, and fearful that an officer might
appear, he withdrew.

This little incident served to make Matt many
friends. People always like to see persons stick up
for their rights, and in this particular case they were
pleased to see the mean store-keeper " talked-down,"
as he well deserved to be.

The album was again put up, and after consider
able talking was knocked down to Podders, the
very individual Isaac Marvelling had endeavored to
persuade away from the sale. Matt purposely let
Podders have the album quite cheaply, and as soon
as it was his Podders declared he would call at
Marvelling's store and see if it could be duplicated
at the price he had paid.

The young auctioneer knew this could not be
done, and he offered to buy the album back at
double the price should Podders succeed.

This pleased the farmer, and also many others,
and, as a consequence, Matt had a brisk run of luck
until closing-up time. The boy felt highly elated,
especially when, on counting up the cash, he found
he had taken in sixteen dollars, one third of which
was profit.

On the following morning another heavy rain
came up, and Matt found it of no advantage to open

up for business. Shortly after dinner Andy came back from New York, and to him Matt related all that had occurred.

"That's right, Matt, always stick up when you are in the right, and you'll come out on top," said the senior partner of the firm.

Andy had struck several decided bargains in goods in the metropolis, and had invested every dollar of available cash. He had had all of the goods shipped to Phillipsburg, the next stopping place, and said they would most likely find them at the freight depot upon their arrival there.

During the afternoon it cleared up, and people began to drift into the shop. Andy opened up the sale, and by evening both of the partners were quite busy. When he went to supper Matt saw Isaac Marveiling, but the store-keeper only favored him with a deep scowl.

"I suppose he would like to chew my head off if he dared," laughed the young auctioneer, as he related the occurrence to Andy.

"No doubt of it, Matt. He feels sore, especially as we are selling just such goods as he has displayed in his window, and at about half the price."

"Well, we won't worry him after to night," smiled Matt, for the start for Phillipsburg was to be made on the following morning.

After closing up the sale that night, the wagon was once more packed, so that they might be on the way at an early hour. The stock on hand was growing lighter, and they were glad to know that more goods would await them upon their arrival

" We are doing famously," remarked Andy. " If we keep on we shall soon be rich."

" I want to pay back Miss Bartlett what she loaned me as soon as I can."

" I reckon she is in no hurry. You had better keep some cash on hand in case of an emergency."

The work of selling goods and packing the wagon had tired Matt considerably, but his mind was too much aroused to go to sleep at once, and so he started out for a short walk before retiring.

He knew very little of the roads around the village, but he was confident that he would not get lost, especially as it was a bright starlight night.

He passed the shop where the sales had been conducted, and then branched off on a road that but a short distance away crossed a tiny brook.

At the brook he paused, and then, struck with a sudden fancy, he left the bridge to go down and bathe his hands and face in the cool, running water.

He had hardly leaped from the bridge to the rocks below when a sudden noise beside him caused him to start back. Almost at the same time a dark form passed under the bridge and was lost to view in the bushes beyond. It looked somewhat like the form of a man, but Matt was not sure.

" That was queer," thought the young auctioneer, as he paused, in perplexity. " Was that a man, or only some animal ?"

Disturbed at the occurrence, Matt leaped up upon the bridge again, without having touched the water. He had hardly come up into the starlight when two men came rushing toward him from the road.

" Who's that ?" cried one of the men.

" That must be the man !" cried the other, and Matt recognized Isaac Marvelling's voice. " Catch hold of him, Jackson."

In another moment the two men stood beside Matt. As he recognized the young auctioneer, Isaac Marvelling set up a cry of surprise and triumph.

" I told you so !" he declared. " I said them auction fellows weren't no better than thieves! This is the chap that broke in my store, Jackson, I feel sure of it ! I want him arrested, and you had better handcuff him so that he can't get away from you! No wonder they can sell cheap, when they steal their goods !"

CHAPTER XXI.

THE TELL-TALE CAP.

For the moment Matt could do little more than stare at the two men that confronted him. In a dim way he realized that Isaac Marvelling's store had been entered and robbed, and that the mean-minded store-keeper fully believed that he was the guilty party.

"Are you a-holding him, Jackson?" went on Isaac Marvelling anxiously. "Look out, or he may slip away from you."

"I've got him, right enough," returned Jackson, one of the local constables. "He'll have hard work to get away."

"What does this mean?" demanded the young auctioneer, aroused at last to the necessity of doing something in his own behalf. "Let go of me!"

"Oh, no, not just yet!" returned Jackson. "You're wanted, and you know it."

"That's right, Jackson, don't let him slip you!" put in Marvelling eagerly. "He's a good talker, but don't let that count with you."

" Will you tell me what I am wanted for?" asked
Matt.

" For entering his store and stealing a lot of cut
lery and jewelry," returned the constable.

" Forty-five dollars' worth," added Marvelling.
" And all new stock, too! Oh, you thought you
would get away with it mighty smart-like, didn't
you?" he sneered.

" I haven't been near your store, and I know
nothing about the theft," was Matt's steady reply.

" But we saw you run away from the store and
come down here, didn't we, Jackson?"

" We certainly did," returned the constable, with
a grave shake of his head.

" You saw me?" gasped Matt, starting back.

" Exactly," said Isaac Marvelling. " I heard you
run out of the yard behind the store right after I
had called in Jackson to tell him about the robbery.
We both saw you jump the fence and skip off in
this direction."

" You might as well own up to what you have
done," added the constable. " It won't do you any
good to deny it."

For the moment Matt did not reply to this. He
was thinking of what had occurred at the bridge
just before the two men had reached it. Could it
be possible that the dark object which had left the

place when he had arrived was the thief, rooted out of what he had considered a safe hiding-place?

" How near were you to me when you saw me first?" he asked of Marvelling.

" We were near enough."

" Did you see my face?"

" Never mind if we did or not."

" No, I must say I didn't see your face," said the constable, who, although a friend of the store-keeper, was yet disposed to be fair and square.

" You probably saw a man, and he ran in this direction," went on Matt.

" We saw you," said Marvelling doggedly. " March him back to the store, Jackson, and we'll make him confess where he has placed the stolen stuff.   He doesn't seem to have it with him."

" If you wish to get back your goods you had better listen to what I have to say," returned Matt, trying to keep down his rising temper.   " I did not enter your store, but perhaps I can put you on the track of the party who did."

" Oh, pshaw ! that's all talk !" snarled Isaac Marvelling.   " March him back, Jackson."

" It won't do any harm to listen to his story," said the constable meekly.   " I reckon you want to get the goods back more than anything."

" Of course ! of course !" responded the store-keeper eagerly. "I can't afford to lose forty-five dollars' worth of stuff at once."

"You say you didn't do the job, and that you think you can put us on the right track?"

"I think I can do something for you," returned Matt.

And in a few brief words he told how he happened to be at the bridge and what he had seen. The constable listened with deep interest, but Isaac Marvelling pooh-poohed the whole story.

"He's a good one at telling 'em," said the storekeeper. "I don't place no credit in what he says."

"Well, it won't do any harm to investigate," replied Jackson. "You hold him, while I light my lantern and take a look under the bridge."

"He may try to get away from me," said Marvelling, as he surveyed Matt's tall and well-built form with some trepidation. "He would most likely do anything to keep out of jail."

"I have more at stake than you have," cried the young auctioneer.

"Indeed?"

"Yes, sir. I consider my reputation worth considerably more than a paltry forty-five dollars."

"Do you? Well, to me the reputation of a traveling and swindling auctioneer isn't worth much!" grumbled Isaac Marvelling.

"You may regret those words," was Matt's brief reply; and for the time being he said no more.

In the meanwhile Jackson had struck a match and lit the somewhat smoky lantern he carried.

Seeing to it that Matt was safe in Marvelling's custody, the constable sprang down from the bridge to the rocks below. A second later he disappeared under the bridge.

The two above heard him rummaging around in the loose stones and among the brush for all of five minutes. Both listened for some call from him, the store-keeper all the while keeping a tight hold on Matt's arm.

"Well, have you found anything?" cried the store-keeper at last, unable longer to stand the suspense.

"I have," returned Jackson, and a second later he appeared again, holding in his hand a carving-knife and two spoons.

"Found these under the bridge," he explained, as he clambered up upon the structure again. "They are your goods, I take it."

"Of course they are my goods!" cried Isaac Marvelling, as he glanced at the articles. "Is that all?" he went on disappointedly.

"That's all I could find. There may be more there or in the water."

"This young rascal threw them there?" cried the store-keeper, shaking Matt's arm savagely. "You imp! tell me where the other things are at once, or I'll skin you alive!"

"Look here, Mr. Marvelling; I want you to let go of me and be reasonable," returned Matt, as calmly as he could. "I am not a thief. If I was, would I tell the story I did, or send down your companion to find those things? My story about that object under the bridge is true, and, to my way of thinking, it was the thief you saw jump the fence and run in this direction. When I sprang down to bathe my face and hands he got scared and ran out on the other side of the bridge, and in his hurry he must have dropped the things which have been found."

"Stuff and nonsense!"

"His story may be true," put in Jackson mildly.

"My advice is to follow up the brook and see if you cannot track the thief," went on the young auctioneer. "And do not lose any time in doing it."

"And what will become of you?" sneered the store-keeper.

"I will go with you, if you wish."

"That's a good idea," said the constable. "Come, let us start without delay. If we can't find anybody we can take the boy to the lock-up, anyway."

Isaac Marvelling grumbled, but at last consented, and soon all three were down under the bridge. Here it was pitch-dark, and the feeble rays of the lantern only lit up a circle that was less than three yards in diameter.

In hopes of clearing himself, more than for the purpose of aiding Isaac Marvelling in the recovery of the goods, Matt set to work with a will.

"Here is another spoon," he said presently, and he handed over a silver-plated affair, which at the most was not worth fifteen cents, wholesale.

"Here are a couple of knives," added Jackson. "And here is a bit of paper some of the stuff must have been wrapped in."

"Look here!" suddenly cried Matt, as he pointed down into the water. "Here's a man's cap, and it looks as if it had just fallen in, for one side of the peak is not yet wet."

"Let me see that cap," returned the constable quickly.

He snatched it from Matt's hand and turned with it to the lantern. His examination lasted but a few seconds.

"Say, Marvelling, have you seen anything of old Joe Yedley lately?" he asked, turning to the store-keeper.

"Yedley! Why, yes; he was in the store beg-

ging, only yesterday," was the reply.   "But what
has he——"

"Did you give him anything?"

"Give him anything?" cried Marvelling wrathfully.   "Not a cent!   I told him to clear out; that
I didn't want him to ever come in again.   I have
no use for beggars."

"Did he go near the case with the cutlery and
jewelry in it?"

"Humph! I suppose he did.   But what has he to
do with this?"

"This is Joe Yedley's cap; I would know it out
of a thousand.   He is an old offender, and it is more
than likely that he is the thief!"

CHAPTER XXII.

THE SHANTY IN THE WOODS.

THE reader may rest assured that Matt listened with deep interest to the words of the constable. He knew nothing of the man that had been mentioned as the probable thief, but he was willing to believe Jackson's supposition true.

"That Joe Yedley's cap?" returned Isaac Marvelling slowly.

"Certainly. You ought to know it well enough. He has worn nothing else for years."

"Humph! how did it get here?"

"The man must have dropped it in his haste to get away when I came here," said Matt. "He left in a big hurry."

"That's most likely it," said the constable. "To tell the truth, it looks just like a piece of Yedley's work," he added slowly. "He did it in order to get square, as much as anything, I reckon. He always resented being called a beggar."

"Humph!" muttered Isaac Marvelling, not par-

ticularly pleased over the turn affairs seemed to be
taking. "He may be guilty and he may not be. I
rather think you had better hold this young fellow
for awhile yet."

"Just as you say."

"You may hold me if you wish," put in the young
auctioneer. "But if you want to get all of your
stuff back you had better follow up this Yedley."

"I'll do that," returned the constable. "I have
an idea I can find out where he has gone to. He
has several old hang-outs here, and most likely he'll
be at one or another of them."

"Are any of the places close at hand?"

"He used to put up at a shanty back here in the
woods," was the slow reply. "It is possible he has
struck for that place—or else for Bill Voegler's
barn."

"Supposing we three make for the shanty without delay?"

The matter was talked over, and finally Isaac
Marvelling, urged on solely by the desire to recover
his goods and not to clear Matt, consented to accompany the others to the place the constable had
named.

It was a dark and lonely road the trio had to
travel. But Jackson knew the way well, and to
avoid suspicion, put out the light. He cautioned

them not to make any noise, and so, as silently as Indians, they filed along, Jackson first and Marvelling last, with the young auctioneer between them.

Ten minutes' walking brought them to the edge of a bit of woodland, surrounded on three sides by corn-fields. Here Jackson called a halt.

"The shanty is not two hundred feet from here. Keep quiet while I go on and investigate," he whispered.

The constable glided out of sight, and five minutes of silent suspense followed.

"It ain't likely he'll find anything," grumbled Isaac Marvelling. "This ain't anything but a wild goose chase."

"Wait," returned Matt. "He must go slow, or he may——"

The young auctioneer broke off short, for at that instant several loud exclamations reached their ears.

"Surrender, Yedley!" they heard Jackson cry. "Surrender, in the name of the law!"

"Who told ye to come here?" yelled the voice of an old man. "Git out an' leave me alone."

"I arrest you, Yedley, for stealing— Hullo! he's gone! Stop him! stop him!"

There was the banging of a shanty door, and

then a crashing in the bushes. Footsteps came close to where Matt and Marvelling stood.

"He's coming this way!" cried the young auctioneer. "Let us stop him!"

"You stop him!" stammered the store-keeper. "He is—is a very ugly man to deal with."

And as the old fellow in question appeared in sight, the store-keeper dropped down behind the rail fence, leaving Matt to face Joe Yedley alone.

This the young auctioneer did without hesitation.

"Stop where you are!" he cried out, and as Yedley attempted to leap the fence, he caught the fellow by the leg and dragged him to the ground.

"Let go of me!" howled the man savagely. "Let go, boy, or it will be the worse for you!"

"Don't you attempt to rise, or I'll knock you down," was Matt's undaunted reply. "Just you remain where you are until Mr. Jackson gets back."

But Yedley would not remain still, and as a consequence, a fierce struggle ensued. Matt called to Isaac Marvelling to come to his assistance, but the store-keeper was too afraid to do so, and only screamed for Jackson to come and secure the thief.

Yedley, although well along in years, was very strong and active, and Matt gradually found himself being overpowered. But he held on until

Jackson arrived, and then the man was quickly subdued by the sight of the constable's pistol.

"Now, Yedley, you had better tell us what you have done with the stolen goods," said Jackson, after he and the others had somewhat regained their breath.

"Yes! yes! hand over my goods!" put in Isaac Marvelling eagerly.

"Ain't got no goods—didn't steal nuthin'!" growled the old man.

"We know better," said Jackson. "We'll search the shanty."

This was done, and in one corner, under some loose flooring, was found a large bundle done up in several newspapers. When this was opened there came to light many knives, forks and spoons, as well as a quantity of cheap jewelry, such as watch chains, rings and trinkets. The entire collection was not worth over fifteen dollars, although Isaac Marvelling stuck to it that the articles had cost him forty-five dollars cash.

After the store-keeper had made certain that all of his goods, with the exception of several cheap spoons, which must have slipped out of the bundle on the way, were safe, all hands made their way back to the village. Yedley begged to be allowed to go, but the constable was firm, and the man was eventually locked up, and later on sent to jail for one year.

Isaac Marvelling was too mean a man to recognize the service Matt had done him, or to apologize for the false charges he had made against the young auctioneer. As soon as he could he got out of Matt's way, and that was about the last the boy saw of him.

But Jackson, the constable, did not hesitate to tell the whole story, and, as a consequence, the people of the village thought less of the mean store-keeper than ever. His trade dropped down daily, until he was at last forced to give up his store and go back to the farm from which he had originally come.

On the following morning Matt and his partner set off bright and early for Phillipsburg. Andy had heard the particulars of Matt's adventures, and he sincerely trusted that neither would have anything further to do with thieves, little dreaming of what fate had in store for them in the near future.

They had done very well in High Bridge, and so took their time to reach the pretty manufacturing town which lies on the east bank of the Delaware. The road was a good one, and on the way they stopped at a farmhouse, where Andy treated the firm, as he termed it, to apple pie and fresh milk. He was going to pay for these articles in cash, but the farmer's wife wished a hat-pin, and gladly took one out of their stock instead.

When they arrived in Phillipsburg they found that their new goods from New York had not yet arrived, but were told that the cases would probably come in on the afternoon freight. After this they started to find a vacant store. Strange to say, there was none to be had which would suit their purpose. There were several large places vacant, but all of them were on side streets, and these they declined to hire.

" We'll have to sell direct from the wagon," said Andy. " Perhaps we'll do just as well."

They found a good corner, and after paying a license fee and getting a square meal, opened up for business. Hardly anything was done during the afternoon, but toward evening trade picked up, and when they finally dismissed the crowd they found they had taken in seventeen dollars.

" And that's pretty good, considering that we are out of many of our best sellers," was Andy's comment. " We must go around to the freight house the first thing in the morning and stock up again."

" I see by the posters that there is to be a big firemen's parade in Easton day after to-morrow," said Matt. " Would it not be a good idea to locate there just before it comes off?"

" Excellent.   Day after to-morrow, you say ?"

" Yes : the posters are everywhere."

" Then instead of remaining here we had better cross the river as soon as we have our cases of goods.   If we can only get a store in a good location we may do better than we did on circus day in those other places."

" That's true, Andy, for I saw by the bills that the railroads are going to run special excursions on account of the big parade, so there will be many strangers with money in the city."

As soon as the freight depot was open the next morning the two drove to the place, and Andy entered the office and called for the cases, three in number.

" What's the name ?" asked the agent in charge.

Andy told him, and an examination of all the freight which had come in was made, and then the two made the dismaying discovery that no goods for them had arrived.

CHAPTER XXIII.

SOMETHING IS MISSING.

"The goods haven't come in!" cried Matt. "What's to be done now? We can't open up without them, and we can't afford to miss the chance of taking a good round sum on parade day."

"I'll telegraph to New York and find out what the trouble is," returned Andy, and he started for the telergaph office without delay.

The message was sent to the metropolis within quarter of an hour, reaching its destination before any of the down-town wholesale houses were open for business. At eleven o'clock a reply came back that the cases had been duly sent, and that the delay would be traced up, if possible, at the freight depot there.

"This leaves us in a pickle for to-day," said Andy, as he handed the message over to Matt.

"Well, it won't be so bad if only we get our goods by to-morrow morning, Andy. Let us go over to Easton, anyway, and look for a store, and if we can find one, take the risk of hiring it."

So they crossed the river and began a search, leaving the horse and wagon tied up at the freight depot in Phillipsburg in the meantime.

They found that the firemen's parade was really to be very large, and already the store-keepers were decorating in its honor. On the streets numerous fakirs were about, offering badges, medals, song-sheets, souvenirs, and other wares for sale.

"I'll take this street, and you take that," said Andy, as they came to a corner. "Go around the block, and then take the next block. In that way we may find a store quicker. There is no use for both of us to go over the same ground."

So, after appointing a meeting-place, the two separated, and Matt hurried along the street Andy had designated to him.

"Here you are, gents, the most wonderful corn and bunion salve in the market!" he presently heard a voice crying out. "Made first expressly for the Emperor of Germany, and now sold in America for the first time. Warranted to cure the worst corn ever known, and sold for the small sum of ten cents! They go like hot-cakes, the boxes do, for they all know how good the salve is! Thank you, sir; who'll have the next?"

Matt stopped short, as something in the voice of the street merchant attracted his attention. He looked at the man and saw that it was Paul Barberry, the fellow who had wished to be taken in as a partner in Newark.

" Give me a box of that ere salve," Matt heard an old man say, and saw the traveling corn doctor hand over a package of his preparation.

The purchaser of the package handed over a quarter of a dollar in silver. Barberry stuck the money in his pocket, and without attempting to give back any change, thrust two more packages of his corn salve into the old man's hands.

" What—what's this?" stammered the old fellow. " Where is my change ?"

" That's all right, three for a quarter, sir," returned Paul Barberry briskly. " Who'll have the next ? Don't all crowd up at once !"

" But I don't want three," said the old man timidly. " I want my change."

" You'll find you need three, find 'em very valuable, sir! That's right, come right up and buy, buy, buy! It's the greatest on the face of the globe !" bawled Barberry, turning away and addressing another crowd on the sidewalk.

" Well, I'll be jiggered !" muttered the old man, and much put out, but too timid to stand up for his rights and demand the return of his money, he placed the packages in his coat-tail pocket, and walked off.

"Well, that's what I call a rather high-handed proceeding," thought Matt. "No wonder some folks consider street merchants and traveling auctioneers little better than thieves, when some of them act in that fashion. I don't think he'll prosper, though, in the end."

He was about to continue on his way, when Paul Barberry caught sight of him and came forward.

"Hullo, my young friend!" he called out pleasantly. "What brings you to Easton—the big parade?"

Matt did not like this manner of being addressed. He considered the corn salve doctor altogether too familiar, so he replied rather coldly:

"Not particularly. We merely struck Easton in the course of our travels."

"Oh, then you and your companion are still on the road with your wagon?"

"Yes."

Paul Barberry seemed to grow interested at once.

"Good enough! And how is business?"

"Very good," returned Matt, and not without pardonable pride.

"Then you are not ready to take me in as a partner yet?"

"Not quite; my friend and I can run the business very well without outside help."

"But you might make more money with me in the firm," went on Paul Barberry persistently.

"We haven't room for a third person."

"Where are you stopping now?"

"We haven't a place yet. My partner and I have just started to look for an empty store."

"Oh, then you are going to stay several days or a week."

"Yes."

"Where were you last?"

"Across the river."

"Do pretty well in Phillipsburg?"

"We did very well—until we began to run out of goods."

"I couldn't do anything in Phillipsburg," grumbled Paul Barberry. "It's only a one-horse place, anyway. So you ran out of goods there?"

"We ran out of some goods—our best sellers."

"Why don't you send for more goods?"

"We have sent, and we are expecting the cases at any moment at the Phillipsburg freight depot."

"Where is your horse and wagon?"

" Tied up at the depot over there," and to avoid
being questioned further, Matt began to move off.

" I think I can get a good store for you," went on
Barberry, catching him by the arm.

" Thank you, but I would prefer to do my own
hunting," returned the young auctioneer, still more
coolly.

" Don't want anything to do with me, eh ?" retorted the corn salve vender angrily.

" I don't want you to take your valuable time in
transacting my business," returned Matt, and off he
hurried, before Barberry could offer any reply.

" He and his partner are mighty independent
chaps," grumbled the pretended doctor, as he gazed
after Matt, with a scowl on his face. " I suppose
he thinks himself above me because he has a horse
and wagon. Well, maybe he won't be any better
off than I am some day."

And, in far from a good humor, Paul Barberry
resumed the sale of his so-styled wonderful corn
cure, a preparation, by the way, which was of no
value as a remedial agent.

Matt walked along for several blocks without
running across any empty stores that would be
suitable for holding sales. Most of the places were
too small, and others were in out-of-the-way corners,

to which it would be next to impossible to attract a crowd.

At the appointed time he walked to the spot where he was to meet Andy. His partner was waiting for him, a smile resting on his pleasant face.

" Any luck, Matt?" he asked.

" None."

" I've struck something that I imagine will just suit us. Come on and look at it."

The two hurried to the place Andy had in mind. It was, indeed, a good store, and just in the right spot, and ten minutes later they were on the way to hunt up the landlord and rent the place.

It was no easy matter to find the person for whom they were seeking, and it was well along in the afternoon before the man who owned the building was found. He agreed to let them have the store for four days for ten dollars, and the bargain was closed on the spot.

Then they returned to the store and cleaned it up as best they could, and at a little after five o'clock locked up and started back to Phillipsburg to ascertain if their cases of goods had yet arrived.

The walk across the bridge did not take long, and the freight depot was close at hand.

" Why, where is the horse and wagon?" cried

Matt, as he discovered that the turn-out was missing from the place where Billy had been fastened.

"Well, that's what I would like to know," returned Andy. "I don't see a thing of it anywhere, do you?"

They looked around, up one street and down another, but neither Billy nor the gayly-painted wagon came into view.

"I'll ask the freight agent about it," said Matt, and he hurried into the office.

"Your horse and wagon?" repeated the agent, in reply to his question. "Why, I guess your man drove off with them."

"Our man?" gasped the young auctioneer.

"Yes; the one you sent around here to get those cases of goods you were expecting. He took the cases, too."

CHAPTER XXIV.

ALONG THE RIVER.

MATT could do nothing but stare at the freight agent. A man had come there and driven off with the horse and wagon and taken the cases of goods with him. It seemed too bold-faced to be true.

"Our man?" he stammered. "We have no man."

"Didn't you send the man here?" demanded the agent, as he stopped short in his work of checking off packages.

"We certainly did not," returned the young auctioneer. "Andy!" he called out, as he stepped back toward the open door, and a moment later Andy Dilks hurried into the depot.

"He says a man came here, got the cases of goods, and drove off with Billy," cried Matt breathlessly. "You did not send any one here, did you?"

"Certainly not," returned Andy promptly. "When was this?"

"Less than two hours ago," replied the freight

agent, and he was now all attention. "Do you mean to say the fellow was a thief?"

" He was!" cried Matt.

"I don't see how he could be anything else," added Andy. "Did he pretend to have an order for the cases?"

" Yes, he had a written order."

"And the bill of lading?"

" N—no, he didn't have that," was the slow reply. " But I thought it was all right. He looked like an honest chap. You had better notify the police at once."

"We will," said Matt. "What sort of a.looking fellow was he?"

As best he could the freight agent gave a description of the man who had driven off with the goods and the turn-out. Matt and Andy both listened attentively.

"By the boots, I'll bet it was that Paul Barberry!" almost shouted the young auctioneer, ere the agent had ceased talking. "This is his way of getting even with us for not taking him into partnership."

" Perhaps you are right," returned Andy. "Did you say anything to him about the wagon being here?"

"I did." And Matt briefly narrated the conversation he had had with the corn doctor.

Then the agent was questioned further, and it was not long before all three were convinced that the pretended doctor was the guilty party.

"If I had known he wasn't square I would not have let him have the cases of goods, that's sure," said the agent meekly.

"I do not doubt that," returned Andy. "But the loss of the horse and wagon is more than we can stand as it is. We will have to hold the railroad responsible for the three cases."

"Can't we go after the thief?" suggested the agent, considerably worried, for he well knew that if the stolen cases were not recovered the loss would come out of his own pocket.

"Have you a horse and wagon?"

"Yes, and I can get it in five minutes."

"What direction did the thief take, do you suppose?"

The freight agent thought for a moment.

"It is my opinion that he either went over to Easton or else up the river."

"It is not likely that he went across the bridge," said Matt. "If it was this Paul Barberry he would be afraid to take that direction, fearing to meet me and my partner on our way here."

"Yes, that's so," put in Andy.

"Then he went up the river. There is quite a good road for a number of miles."

"Well, supposing you get your horse and wagon," said Matt impatiently. "It will not do to waste time here."

"But what of the police?" questioned Andy.

"We can notify them when we come back—that is, if we are unsuccessful."

"All right; hurry up that wagon, then."

The freight agent at once disappeared around the corner of the building. He was gone nearly five minutes. When he returned he was leading a fine black horse, attached to a light road wagon.

"Brought you Flip, my fast trotter," he explained. "He ought to be able to overtake any bit of horse-flesh in these parts."

"Well, we want a fast horse," replied Matt, as he sprang into the wagon without delay. He was quickly followed by Andy and the freight agent, and off they went at a spanking gait down the smooth road.

It was a fine day, cool and clear, and under any other circumstances both Matt and Andy would have enjoyed the drive. But just now they were filled with fears. Supposing they were unable to recover their turn-out and goods what then?

The partners looked at each other, and that look

meant but one thing. They must recover their property. Such a thing as failure was not to be countenanced.

At length Phillipsburg was left far behind, and they entered a somewhat hilly farming section. Presently they came to a farmhouse standing close to the road. There was an old countryman standing by the gate, smoking a pipe leisurely, and Matt directed the freight agent to draw rein.

"Good afternoon," said the young auctioneer politely. "I wish to ask you for a bit of information."

"Well, son, what is it?" returned the old countryman, removing his pipe from his mouth and gazing at all three curiously.

"Did an auction wagon pass this way a short while ago?"

"An auction wagon?"

"Yes, sir, a covered wagon, with the sign, 'Eureka Auction Co.,' painted on the sides. It had a single white horse, with brown spots."

The old man's face lit up.

"Oh, yes; I saw that wagon," he replied.

"You did?" cried Andy. "We are very glad to hear it. Which way did it go?"

"Right up that way," and the countryman waved his hand to the northwest.

"Along the river still," said the freight agent. "I thought so."

He was about to drive on when Matt stopped him.

"Did you notice who was driving the wagon?" he called back.

"Yes, a tall man kind of shabbily dressed."

"Must be Barberry," muttered the young auctioneer.

"What's the trouble?" questioned the countryman curiously.

"The turn-out has been stolen, that's the trouble," replied the boy, and off they sped again, leaving the old countryman staring after them in open-mouthed wonder.

They turned from the main road, which about half a mile back had led away from the Delaware, and took the side road the old man had indicated. It was an uneven wagon track, and they went bumping over rocks and stumps of trees in a most alarming fashion.

"He couldn't have gone far in this direction," muttered the freight agent ruefully. "Why, it is enough to break the springs of any wagon ever made."

"My idea is that he had an object in coming down here," responded Andy thoughtfully. "Is there any sort of bridge in the neighborhood?"

The agent shook his head.

" No."

" Or a place where the river might be forded?"

" Not now. The heavy rains have swollen the stream, as you can see. In real dry weather he might find a place to ford."

" Well, it's certain that if he came this way to merely get out of our reach he chose an awful way of doing it," remarked Matt, as a sudden lurch of the wagon sent him bouncing up into the air. " This is the worst riding I've struck yet."

" Worse than when Billy ran away?" questioned Andy, with a sudden gleam of humor.

" Well, hardly that," admitted the young auctioneer. " But that wasn't riding at all. That was a slap-bang, go-as-you-please trip, which didn't— hullo ! look there !"

He motioned to the freight agent to draw rein and pointed to a deep track in a soft bit of ground ahead.

" It's the track of our wagon sure enough !" exclaimed Andy. " I could tell it out of a hundred."

" So could I, Andy. Follow that, please," went on Matt, to the agent.

" It's queer you didn't see that track before," said the driver slowly.

" The reason is because it comes from the rocks.

Barberry thought it best to keep on the rocks, I
suppose. Maybe he thought he would get stuck in
the mud with the cases if he got on soft ground."

"That's the truth of it, you can depend on it,"
said Andy. "Hurry up and follow that track to
the end, and we'll soon have our wagon and goods
back."

On and on they went, over soft patches of ground,
through low bushes, and around rocks and fallen
trees. Sometimes they were close to the water's
edge, and again they traveled almost out of sight of
the clear-flowing stream.

"We can't go much further in this direction,"
said the freight agent, when all of a mile of ground
had been covered.

"Why not?" asked Andy.

"There is a big wall of rock just ahead. We will
have to pull away from the river now."

"No, we won't!" shouted Matt. "Look there!"

And he pointed to where the wagon tracks led
directly down into the water.

"I'll bet all I am worth that he crossed the stream
here," he went on. "Do you not see how shallow
it is? He went over to that island, and from there
directly to the other side."

CHAPTER XXV.

A BITTER MISTAKE.

Both Andy and the freight agent saw at once that Matt was right, and the jaw of the driver of the wagon dropped.

"Humph! I was certain he couldn't cross right after such heavy rains," he said moodily.

"But you see he has crossed," went on the young auctioneer. "I will tell you what I'm going to do —wade across and see if I can't strike the tracks on the other side."

"You'll get pretty wet, especially if you slip into a deep hole," returned Andy.

"I'll take off part of my clothing," returned Matt, and he did so without delay.

The water was colder than he had anticipated, and he shivered slightly as he waded in deeper and deeper.

"Can you swim, should you slip?" called out Andy anxiously.

" Yes, I can swim," returned Matt, " but I hope that won't be necessary !"

Moving along cautiously where the rocks stuck up the highest, the young auctioneer worked his way slowly over to the island he had previously pointed out. It was painful work, for he had taken off his shoes, and now he found the bottom in many places cut his feet. But at last the island was reached, and he walked out upon the dry ground.

It did not take Matt long to discover the wagon tracks for which he was searching. They were close at hand, and led almost in a straight line across the little patch, which was not over two hundred feet in width.

"Here they are !" he shouted back to the others. " He went right across just as I supposed."

" Humph ! Now what is to be done ?" questioned the agent, with a perplexed look upon his face.

" We must cross and follow him," replied Andy determinedly.

" Do you want me to take the horse and wagon across ?"

" Why not ? The thief took that heavily loaded wagon over. I guess this light affair will go over all right."

The agent was doubtful about this, and rubbed his chin reflectively.

" I might drive on till I got to a bridge, or turn back to one," he suggested.

" That would take too long," returned Matt's partner impatiently. " We must ' strike while the iron is hot,' as the saying is."

" Come on !" shouted Matt from the island. " Come straight over and you will be all right."

" Well, we can make the venture, but I am a bit shaky over it," said the freight agent, and with a face full of the concern he felt for his turn-out he headed his trotter toward the water.

At first the horse was inclined to shy to one side. He pranced up and down a bit and dug into the sand and loose stones with his hoofs.

" You can see he don't want to go," said the driver. " I really think we had better find a bridge."

" Oh, nonsense! give me the reins!" returned Andy sharply, seeing that the fellow was altogether too easily frightened. " I will take him over safely."

" Don't be too sure!" cried the agent in alarm. " He will break at the least little thing !"

But Andy would not listen to him further. He

took the reins, and holding them firmly, tapped the trotter with the whip.

The horse made a rush into the water, and in less than ten seconds the wagon was in up to the axles.

"We will be drowned! We will be drowned!" cried the agent in sudden terror. "I can't swim!"

"We won't be drowned. Just you hold on and keep quiet," returned Andy shortly.

"But—but we are going deeper!"

"Not much deeper. I can still see the bottom."

"Supposing we should slip—or Flip should slip?"

"Or we had an earthquake," added Andy, utterly disgusted with the freight agent's actions. "Don't you want to get back those cases, or do you prefer to pay for them?"

This last remark effectually silenced the man. He clung to the seat looking badly scared, but he offered no more suggestions.

With due caution, but as rapidly as possible, Andy drove the horse over the rocks, carefully avoiding such spots as he thought might be extra deep or slippery. Matt, on the island, shouted several directions to him; and thus the journey was safely accomplished.

"Good so far!" cried the young auctioneer, when the horse was once more on dry ground. "That was easy enough."

"Easier than I thought it would be!" exclaimed the freight agent, with a deep breath of relief. "I wish we were over all the way!"

"The second trip will be easier than the first was," remarked Andy. "It is much more shallow."

"I will wade ahead and make sure of the way," put in Matt, and without loss of time he started out.

It was not so deep toward the Pennsylvania shore, but the current appeared to run swifter, and the boy had all he could do when up to his thighs to keep his feet. But the horse and wagon came along all right, and inside of ten minutes they were high and dry upon the opposite bank.

Here it did not take long to rediscover the tracks made by the auction turn-out, and as soon as Matt could don what clothing he had taken off, they started to follow it up once more.

"I can't see why he crossed the river in that fashion," grumbled the freight agent, as he tapped his horse with the whip.

"I can," returned Andy. "He did it to throw us off the track. He had no time to get rid of the signs on the wagon, and he knew we would learn, sooner or later, in what direction he had gone. But he thought we would not find out how he had crossed and would think that he had kept along on the eastern bank."

On and on they went, over the rocky roads, now through a sharp cut between the mountains, and then again around a curve overlooking some tiny stream far below.

" A beautiful place," said Matt, as his eyes rested on a particularly beautiful bit of picturesque scenery. " How can people stick in the stuffy city when there is so much like this going to waste, so to speak?"

" That's a conundrum," returned Andy. " But I have heard it said that many city-born folks would rather die between brick walls than live amid green fields."

" Just look at those rocks and trees, and listen to those birds sing!"

" It is truly grand, that's a fact," returned Andy. " Do you know, if I was wealthy, I believe I would like nothing better than to spend all of my summer in among the mountains."

" And that would just suit me," returned Matt enthusiastically, and then he suddenly sobered down. " But we are not rich, Andy, and unless we get back our turn-out we'll be as poor as ever."

" Oh, we'll have to catch that thief," put in the freight agent. " He can't be many miles ahead."

" The trouble is it's growing dark, and we can

hardly see the wagon tracks any more," said the young auctioneer.

" It grows dark early in among the mountains," remarked Andy. " If the land was level, it would be light enough."

On they went, passing through several little hamlets. At each of these places they inquired about the auction wagon, and were told that it had passed through, the man driving at almost top speed.

" He is going to get away as far as he can before he puts up for the night," said Andy. " I do not believe we will catch him until we reach the place at which he is stopping."

" My trotter is not used to this sort of thing," said the freight agent. " He is beginning to play out."

" At the next town we reach we can hire a horse," said Matt. " And you can go back if you wish. There is no telling how long this chase may last."

" I ought to be back attending to business," was the agent's reply. " My clerk can hardly take my place. Would you two be willing to go on alone?"

"Certainly," returned Andy.

The next place, a village of perhaps twenty or thirty houses and half a dozen stores, was soon reached. There was a small tavern, and they drove up to this. Alighting, Matt ran inside and ques-

tioned the half a score of loungers concerning the
auction wagon.

Every man in the place shook his head. The
wagon had not been seen in the village. Nearly all
of the men had just come in from work, and every
one said that had the wagon been on the main road
at all he would have seen it.

Matt listened with a sinking heart, and as Andy
came in he grasped his parter by the shoulder.

"We have made a mistake," he said faintly.

"A mistake, Matt?"

"Yes. The wagon did not come here at all. We
are on the wrong track!"

CHAPTER XXVI.

SOMETHING OF A SURPRISE.

ANDY was certainly as much dismayed as Matt at the discovery which had been made. Just at the time when they supposed that they were drawing closer to the object of their chase, they found that they were most likely further away than ever. The older member of the firm gave another groan, and this was supplemented by another from the freight agent.

" I knew he couldn't cross that river," growled the latter. " Now, just see what a wild goose chase you have led us !"

" Oh, he crossed the river, there is no doubt of that !" returned Matt quickly. " But where we got off the track was somewhere among the mountains. We dropped the right track and took something that resembled it."

" Yes, that must be the truth of the matter," put in Andy. " It's too bad !"

"What's it all about, anyway?" questioned the tavern-keeper curiously.

In a few brief words Andy explained matters, while not only the tavern-keeper, but also the others in the place, listened with deep interest.

"Any reward offered for catching the rascal?" questioned one of the men present, a brawny individual—evidently a mountaineer.

"Yes," returned Matt quickly. "How much shall we offer, Andy?" he asked in a whisper.

"Twenty-five dollars would not be too much," returned his partner. "It is quite a sum to us, I know, but I guess we would rather have our turn-out back a dozen times over."

"We will give twenty-five dollars in cash for the return of our horse, wagon and goods," said Matt, in a voice loud enough for all to hear.

"Twenty-five dollars in cash!" repeated several, and it was plain to see that this offer was regarded as quite liberal.

"What kind of a looking turn-out is it?" was next asked.

Matt described Billy and the wagon. All listened attentively, and when he had finished the mountaineer who had first spoken tapped him on the shoulder.

"I'll go out with ye and hunt him up, stranger."

"So will I!" cried another.

"And I!" added a third, and soon six men stood ready to continue the search with Andy and Matt.

Seeing this, the freight agent decided to drive back home, taking a much better road, which led down to Easton. He did not lose any time in starting, and, if the truth must be told, both Andy and Matt were glad to be rid of him.

After he had gone the auctioneers procured another horse and wagon from the tavern-keeper and also a couple of lanterns. The mountaineer had a mule upon which he rode, and the other men went along on foot.

They traveled the road by which the young auctioneers had come. The village was situated in a small open spot, and now, when they once more found themselves between the mountains, they were enveloped in a darkness which the rays of the lanterns scarcely dispersed.

They traveled along as rapidly as possible, and inside of half an hour came to a fork in the road which Matt had had in mind since the discovery of their mistake had been made.

"We will examine the ground here," he said. "It is more than likely he branched off here."

He was soon hard at work, and all of the others with him. The wagon track they had followed was very plainly to be seen, and now Matt saw, at a spot which was covered with loose stones, where the thief had branched off with his stolen outfit.

"That is the road he took," he announced to the others. "Had we followed him from here in the first place we would most likely have caught up to him by this time."

"Is that 'ere track the right one?" questioned the mountaineer eagerly.

"I believe it is."

"Then I'm off fer the reward!" shouted the brawny fellow. "Git up, Bones!" and he slapped the mule with the flat of his hand, and was off without another word.

"Ramson will get it, sure," grumbled one of the other men. "No use for us to go any further."

And he turned on his heel and started back for the village, followed by most of the others, leaving a single man to race after the mountaineer on foot.

Matt and Andy were not slow to urge their fresh horse forward. But the way was now even darker than before and also rougher, and it was with difficulty that the wagon moved along.

"I don't believe he went very far on this road," said Matt, bringing the horse to a halt. "I am going to follow that track on foot."

He sprang down from the seat, and with the light

close to the ground, moved along in front of the
horse. It was well that he did so, for hardly had
he advanced a hundred feet than he uttered a cry
and came to a halt.

" What's up now ?" questioned Andy, peering forward through the gloom.

" He turned off here and went into the brush on
the left. Don't you see the tracks?"

" But there is no road through the brush. He
would lose his way and get caught among the rocks
further back."

" I have an idea that he drove away in here to
hide the wagon," suddenly cried Matt. " He could
very well do that, you know, and then ride off on
horseback to some place and put up for the night."

" By the boots, I believe you are right !" returned
Andy. " Why, of course that is just what he has
done ! How stupid of us not to think of that before."

" I hope the wagon is still O. K.," went on Matt.
" It would be hard work to get a spring fixed in this
out-of-the-way place."

" Well, we must find the wagon first. Supposing
we tie up and go ahead on foot."

" I'm willing."

They were soon side by side, making their way

through the brush and around the rocks as rapidly as they could.

" Let us go forward as silently as possible!" suddenly whispered the boy. " Barberry may still be around, and if that is so we want to surprise him."

"That's a good idea! What a pity we can't put out the light."

" We can't do without it. The track is growing fainter. We are coming to almost solid rock."

On and on they pushed, until Andy calculated that they had covered a distance of five hundred feet from the main road. Then they found themselves on the verge of a deep ravine, with a high wall of rock to the left of them.

" Phew! supposing he drove over that!" shuddered Andy, as he pointed into the blackness of the hollow. " That must be a hundred feet or more deep."

" He went to the right, Andy—the only way he could go. Have you any matches with you?"

" Yes. What do you want of them?"

" I am going to put out the light, for I fancy the wagon is not far off, and the thief may be around also. If we wish we can light up again later on."

Matt did as he had intimated, and the two found themselves in a darkness that was simply intense to the last degree. They could not see their hands before their faces, and had to literally feel their way along.

Matt went first, with his partner holding on to the hem of his jacket. They had progressed but a dozen feet when, on rounding a high rock, the young auctioneer stopped once more.

"I was right," he whispered. "The wagon is directly ahead."

"How do you know?"

"I can see the lantern, which is standing on the seat."

"Then the thief must still be around," returned Andy excitedly.

"I suppose so, but I don't see any one. Come on, but don't make any noise, or he may run away, and I think he ought to be captured and locked up."

"Certainly he ought to be placed under arrest. I am ready. Won't he be surprised when he sees us!"

Once again they moved forward toward where the auction wagon stood beneath the shelter of a large tree. Matt noted that Billy had been unharnessed and was tied to the rear, where he was engaged in making a meal of some feed which had been given him.

"Barberry is making himself at home evidently,"

murmured the young auctioneer to himself. "That fellow certainly has nerve!"

"Hold up!" suddenly cried Andy, catching the boy by the arm.

"What's up, Andy?"

"Look there, to your right!"

Matt did as directed, and saw a sight which both amazed and alarmed him. There, by a little fire built to keep them comfortable in the night air, sat two burly men, drinking and smoking. Neither of the individuals was Paul Barberry.

CHAPTER XXVII.

TIMELY ASSISTANCE.

"Those fellows must be the thieves," whispered Andy, as he pointed to the pair beneath the tree.

"I believe you are right," returned Matt. "If so, we have made a big mistake. Neither of them is Paul Barberry, and I was almost certain he was the thief."

"So was I, Matt. But never mind that now. What worries me is the fact that there are two of them."

"Yes, and they both look like strong fellows," returned the young auctioneer, as he surveyed the pair. "If they get ugly when we claim the turn-out we may have a lively time with them."

"Well, we are in the right, and we must stick up for our own."

"Of course we'll do that," cried Matt determinedly. "But I say, wouldn't it be best if we each got a stout stick? They may show fight if they fancy we are beyond outside aid."

" Perhaps we can bluff them into believing that we have the village authorities at our back," suggested Andy. "I would rather frighten them off than run the risk of coming off second best in a set-to with them."

"Hi! what are you fellows doing here?" suddenly demanded a voice just behind Andy. "Do you belong—what, you?"

And the speaker, none other than Paul Barberry, stepped back in amazement.

"What's the trouble there, Barberry?" cried one of the men by the fire, and both sprang up in alarm.

"Why, here are the—the—a couple of young fellows," stammered the corn salve doctor. He was so surprised he could hardly speak. "How did you get here?" he asked slowly.

"Never mind that," returned Matt. "I imagine you know what we are here for."

"No, I don't."

"Really!" returned Andy sarcastically. "Well, then, let me tell you that we came for our horse and wagon and stock."

"I haven't anything of yours," returned Paul Barberry, gradually recovering from his surprise. In making a circle around the improvised camp he had stumbled upon them quite unexpectedly. "You talk as if I was a thief."

"Didn't you run off with that horse and wagon?" demanded Matt.

"Run off with it? No, why should I? The outfit belongs to me. Isn't that so, boys?" and the corn salve doctor turned to his burly companions.

"Why, of course it does!" returned the men.

A thunderbolt from the sky at that moment would not have taken Andy and Matt more by surprise than did this statement. Paul Barberry's assurance actually staggered them, and neither could speak for the moment.

"That outfit belongs to you?" cried Matt at length.

"Of course."

"That's the biggest falsehood I ever heard in my life!" burst out Andy. "You know very well that everything there belongs to us."

"I know no such thing," returned Barberry coldly. "I bought the outfit from you, and you know it. These gentlemen know it also."

And he waved his hand toward his companions.

"Certainly, we know all about it," said one of the men.

"Yes, we saw the money paid over," added the second fellow.

Matt and Andy looked at each other. Each knew very well that the other had never made any bargain for the sale of the turn-out and stock. The whole scheme was one of the corn doctor to get possession of their belongings.

"See here, Barberry, there is no use for you to talk in this fashion," went on Matt, as calmly as he could, although he was worked up to the top notch of excitement. "You know very well that you are asserting that which is not true. The outfit belongs to us, and you haven't the shadow of an interest in it. You stole it from the Phillipsburg freight depot, and——"

"Stop that!" blustered the corn salve doctor. "How dare you call me a thief, boy?"

"That is what you are, and nothing less. If you——"

"Do you hear that, fellows?" interrupted Barberry, turning to the two men.

"You want to keep a civil tongue in your head, boy!" cried one of the men sharply. "Calling a man a thief is a serious business."

"And being a thief is still more serious," replied Andy. "Perhaps you fancy you can bluff us, as the saying is, but you are mistaken. This turn-out is ours, and we are here to claim it. If you molest us in the least we will hand you all over to the police."

"We can stand up for ourselves," returned the

man with a deep scowl. "We are three to two, and we are armed."

"So you would use force to retain our property, eh?" said Andy.

"We do not admit that it is your property."

"But it is. Now let me tell you something. We stopped at the village just north of here, and got the assistance of nearly a dozen men. They are scattered about, and should you attempt to molest us I shall give them a signal——"

"Not much you won't!" cried the man addressed, and springing forward, he clapped his hand over Andy's mouth. "Tend to the other one, fellows, I can manage this one!"

"All right," returned his companion, and he, as well as Paul Barberry, fell upon Matt.

The attack had been so sudden that Andy and Matt were hardly prepared to defend themselves. The former was forced over on his back, and despite his utmost exertions, was unable to remove his assailant's hand from his mouth.

Matt was thrown over on his side, and while Paul Barberry held one of his arms, the other man tried to force him into silence.

"Make a single sound and I'll kick you in the face," he ejaculated in a low, but intense tone.

"Help! help!" cried Matt, ignoring the threat

entirely, and he continued to call out so long as his breath lasted.

The burly ruffian tried to kick him as he had promised, but with his disengaged hand Matt caught his foot, and after dancing about to regain his balance, the man came down heavily across the young auctioneer's legs.

The force of the fall was so great that Matt cried out shrilly with pain. For the moment he imagined that both of his limbs must be broken.

"Clap your hand over his mouth, Barberry!" cried the burly man, as he struggled to regain his feet. "Confound you, boy, I'll teach you to throw me!"

He sprang at Matt, but not before the young auctioneer had had a chance to turn over and spring up. Matt realized what was at stake, and knew he must fight his best or the worst would happen.

Before the man could touch him Matt placed Barberry between them. Then he gave the corn doctor a push that sent him staggering up against his companion.

In the meantime, poor Andy was still flat on his back, unable to speak or to move. His assailant was on top of him, and there did not appear to be any immediate relief in sight.

Seeing this, Matt, as soon as he had freed himself, leaped to his partner's assistance. He caught the ruffian by the shoulders, and with a sharp jerk sent him sprawling flat upon his back on a number of sharp stones.

"Go at them with stones, Andy," shouted Matt, as he himself stooped to pick up a small rock which lay at his feet. "We ought to show them no mercy!"

"That's true," panted his partner as he followed the suggestion by arming himself with several handy missiles. "They are a set of cowards in my opinion."

"We'll show you if we are!" cried the fellow who had first attacked Matt. "Come on, Barberry, we must make them prisoners!"

And once more he sprang forward, while the fellow on his back, with a groan of pain, staggered up to lend his assistance in the struggle.

But now came help for Matt and Andy from an unexpected quarter. There was a crashing through the brush, and a tall form the thieves did not recognize burst into view. It was Ramson, the mountaineer.

"Wot's a-going on here, anyway?" shouted the mountaineer in a tone of wonder. "Fighting worse nor a lot of bears, I declare! Wot's it all about?"

"Help us, won't you?" cried Matt. "These are

the fellows who stole the turn-out, and they will not give it up."

" Won't, hey? Well, it's your'n, ain't it?"

" It certainly is, and if you will help us you shall have that reward," put in Andy. " This is the main thief, and the other two are helping him," and he pointed to Paul Barberry.

Without more ceremony, the tall mountaineer strode forward and caught Barberry by the shoulder and gave him such a twist about that the pretended doctor howled with pain.

"These two young men are honest fellows, I take it," he said. "And if you imagine you can do them out of their rights you are mistaken, at least so long as I am around. Now just you stand still while I attend to your helpers, and I'll—hullo! if they ain't gone and run away !"

Ramson was right. Hardly had he made his little speech than Paul Barberry's two companions had taken time by the forelock and made a rush for the brush. Matt and Andy dashed after them, but it was useless, for a few seconds later they disappeared in the darkness.

CHAPTER XXVIII.

BACK TO THE VILLAGE.

"NEVER mind, let them go," said Andy, as he saw the mountaineer make a movement as if to follow the retreating pair. "I do not think that they have any of the stolen things in their possession."

"But they ought to be locked up," insisted Ramson. "Such thieves ought never to be allowed their liberty."

"I agree with you, but as matters stand, we cannot bother to follow them just now."

"Maybe this fellow will tell us who they were. I didn't get a square look at them," went on the mountaineer, who felt sore to think the pair had gotten away thus easily.

"Yes, I imagine we can learn from Barberry who they are," put in Matt, as he caught the pretended doctor by the arm. "Don't you try to run," he added.

Paul Barberry appeared greatly disconcerted.

He had not expected this sudden turn of affairs, and he knew not what to say or do.

"March him up to the wagon and light the other lantern," said Andy. "I see the fire is going out."

"I'll soon fix that," returned Ramson, and he threw on some dry twigs, causing the fire to blaze up merrily. "They were making themselves quite at home."

"What are you going to do with me?" asked Barberry sullenly, as he found himself surrounded, with no hope of escape.

"Before we answer that question we wish to ask a few on our account," returned Andy. "Now tell us who your companions were."

"A couple of tramps I picked up in Phillipsburg."

"Tramps?"

"That is what I call them. They were bound for Easton to sell prize packages of toilet soap."

"Fakirs, like yourself," put in Matt. "How did you come to pick them up? Were you afraid to steal the outfit alone?"

"I didn't say I stole the outfit."

"No, but you did, nevertheless. Now, how did you happen to fall in with those fakirs?"

"Will you let me go if I tell you?"

"Certainly not," cried the boy. "We intend to

put you where you will not be able to steal any
more for some time to come."

" Arrest me ?" exclaimed Paul Barberry, in great
alarm. Evidently he had not thought such a thing
at all likely.

" Yes," put in Andy. " And unless you do as we
wish you to it may go mighty hard with you."

" But I'll stick to it that I bought the turn-out,"
returned the corn salve doctor, trying to put on a
bold front. " You'll have to prove that you didn't
make the sale. I won't be bulldozed."

"Get a rope and bind him, Matt," said Andy,
paying no attention to the last remark. " We'll
take him to the nearest police station. I suppose
there will have to be some papers made out before
he can be taken back to New Jersey."

The young auctioneer sprang into the wagon and
soon brought forth a long and stout rope. Paul
Barberry watched these preparations with an
anxious face, and when Ramson stepped forward
to aid in making him a close prisoner he began to
wilt.

" See here," he said, addressing Andy and Matt,
" I don't want to be locked up. It would injure my
reputation to a great extent. I am willing to admit
that I have done wrong, but I—I—did it by mistake. I haven't felt well for several days, and my

head has been affected, that's the whole truth of the matter. When I get those spells I don't know what I am doing."

"He's a good one at crawling," remarked Ramson in disgust. "He'll get over the spells when he's locked up.'

In spite of his protestations and pleadings, Barberry was tightly bound and fastened to the rear of the wagon. Then Billy, who had had quite a rest, was harnessed up once more, and with Matt on the seat and Ramson going on ahead to pick the way, they started off for the village, Andy keeping in the rear to see to it that their prisoner should not escape.

The way was dark and uncertain, but the tall mountaineer proved a good and careful guide, and at the end of an hour and a half the worst part of the journey was over. They entered the village just as the town clock was striking one.

"If you want the man arrested you had better take him directly to Justice Harwig's house," said Ramson. "He does all the law business in these parts."

So to that individual's cottage they turned, and Matt sprang from the wagon and used the old-fashioned knocker vigorously. A long silence followed, and then a window upstairs was raised and a head adorned with a nightcap was thrust out.

" What's wanted ?"

" We've got a criminal for ye, judge," called out Ramson. " The fellow as run away with that auction turn-out."

" A criminal, eh? All right, I'll be down in a minnit !"

The head disappeared and the window was closed. Five minutes passed and then a light appeared in a wing of the house, and the justice opened the door to what he termed his office.

" Now, what's it all about ?" he asked in a sleepy voice.

All hands entered the place, Andy and the mountaineer leading Paul Barberry, who looked anything but comfortable. The prisoner was marched up before the justice's desk, and the others ranged themselves alongside of him, while Justice Harwig, a very pleasant man, made himself comfortable to listen to what all hands might have to say.

The hearing was a short one, and at its conclusion Paul Barberry was marched off to the village lock-up, the justice stating that he would notify the Phillipsburg authorities, so that they could get the necessary papers and take him away.

Barberry did all he could to beg off, offering at

the last moment to pay a fine equal to the amount
of money in his pocket—eighteen dollars. But
neither the justice nor the others would listen to
this. Had he not made the fight, Matt and Andy
might have had some pity on him, but they were
but human and could not so easily forget the blows
they had suffered at the hands of the thieves.

It was not deemed worth while to send out any
one to look for the two men who had escaped, and
after Barberry was safe in jail the young auctioneers drove over to the tavern and put up there for
the night. Ramson accompanied them, and before
parting with the mountaineer they paid him the
reward that had been promised, for which he was
very thankful.

On the following morning Matt and Andy lost
no time in starting back for Easton, telling Justice
Harwig that they would report to the authorities in
Phillipsburg whenever wanted. They found that
the turn-out had suffered no damage by being stolen.
The new goods which had been in the cases had
been stored away in some confusion, but Andy soon
straightened this out.

"I tell you we can consider ourselves very lucky
to get out of this so nicely," he said, after he had
finished his work and knew all was right. "As it
stands, we will be out hardly a cent."

"Yes, we were lucky," returned Matt. "But we wouldn't have been had we taken that freight agent's advice and remained on the other side of the Delaware."

"Well, no doubt he'll be glad to learn that we have recovered the goods. It saves him something like seventy-eight dollars.'"

"We will lose the best part of to-day's trade, for we won't be able to get back much before two or three o'clock."

"Never mind, the city is full of people, and we ought to do best in the evening," replied Andy.

It was a cool, clear day, and although both were rather tired from the adventures of the night before, they enjoyed the drive back to Easton. At first Andy drove, while Matt took it easy on the goods in the back of the wagon, and when half the distance was covered the partners changed places, so that by the time the store they had previously hired was reached, both were sufficiently rested to go ahead with the duties on hand.

They lost no time in transferring the stock to the store shelves, after which Andy drove off with the wagon and found a stable where the turn-out might be put up during their stay. Matt arranged the stock on the shelves, and made a great window display. The red flag was hung out, and inside of an hour afterward business was in full swing.

CHAPTER XXIX.

UNDESIRABLE CUSTOMERS.

AMONG their customers they numbered a great
many fire laddies, and these they made it a point to
treat extra well, selling them goods at almost cost.
As a consequence the firemen told their friends, and
by eight o'clock that evening the store was packed.

"This is going to be the banner day after all,"
whispered Andy, just after making several good
sales. "I believe we can keep things moving until
midnight."

They found a great demand for pocket-knives
and cheap jewelry, and by playing on the instruments they sold over three dozen mouth harmonicas
and three accordions. Then Andy and Matt gave
a duet on the violin and banjo, and as a consequence, sold both of the instruments they had
handled.

The music had attracted even a greater crowd,
and among the people were four tall and rather
ugly-looking colored men. They shoved their way

forward rudely, causing some timid customers to leave in a hurry, and then began to laugh and joke among themselves in a loud and coarse manner.

"I am afraid we are going to have trouble with those chaps," whispered Matt to his partner. "They have been drinking, and they are out for a lark."

"That's my idea, too," returned Andy. "We must watch them closely."

For a few minutes the young auctioneers paid no attention to the four negroes, excepting to see that they did not take up something without laying it down again. The fellows moved around through the crowd, and at length two of them leaned up heavily against one of the show-cases which belonged to the store fixtures.

The combined weight of the two men was too much for the top glass of the case, and with a sharp crack it broke into half a dozen pieces.

"Hullo! dat glass dun gone and got broke!" cried one of the negroes. "I wonder how dat happened?"

"You broke that glass!" exclaimed Matt sharply. "You and your companion."

"Me!" returned the offender in pretended surprise.

"Yes, you—and your friend."

" Dat ain't so at all, boss! We didn't touch dat yere glass. Did we, Jeff?"

"'Deed we didn't, Tooker."

" We didn't come in here to do no kind ob damage, boss."

" Never mind what you came in for," returned Matt. " You broke the glass and you will have to pay for it."

At the young auctioneer's statement the faces of all four of the colored men took on a savage look. They had drifted in to do pretty much as they pleased, and had not expected to meet with such strong and sudden opposition.

" I won't pay for nuffin!" growled the ringleader of the quartet. " I dun reckon somebody else in the crowd broke the glass."

" Cos da did," replied another of the colored men. " Maybe yo' think yo' kin lay it on us just because we is colored, hey?"

" Not at all; a colored man can be as much of a gentleman as any one—if he wishes to be," put in Andy.

" Do youse mean to insinuate dat we ain't gen'men?" questioned one of the crowd roughly.

" You are not gentlemen when you break glass and refuse to pay for it," returned Andy. " That

glass is worth at least a dollar, and unless it is paid
for, somebody will be handed over to the police."

"Huh! do yo' fink yo' kin scare us, boss?"

"Yo' say another word an' we'll do up de hull
place!"

"We is as good as any white trash, remember
dat!"

In the meantime one of the colored men slid his
hand into the show-case which had been damaged,
and essayed to grab a small box of watch-chains
which rested close by. Matt saw the movement,
slick as it was, just in time, and springing forward
he caught the colored man by the arm.

"Drop that box!" he cried sternly.

"Oh, I wasn't gwine to take de box," returned
the would-be offender. "I was jess gwine to look
at yo' stock. How much is dem chains worth?"

"I am not selling chains to you to-night," re
turned Matt.

He had hardly spoken when Andy leaned over
his shoulder and whispered into his ear:

"Talk to them for a few minutes, and I'll slip
out and notify the police. Treat them well until I
get back."

And the next instant Matt's partner had disappeared into the crowd, without any of the colored
men noticing his departure.

" Yo' don't want to sell me any chain?" repeated the colored man.

" Not to-night."

" Why not?"

" This isn't chain night. I'm selling harmonicas and banjos."

" Well, let's see some banjos den," put in another of the negroes, and he winked at his companions, thinking that Matt had become too scared to refer to the broken show-case again.

" All right, but I don't want any more show-cases broken," returned the young auctioneer.

He took a banjo from one of the cases and began to tune it up slowly.

" Kin yo' play us a jig?" asked one of the colored men, while the white people in the place looked on in wonder at the turn affairs had taken.

" Oh, yes, I can play a jig," returned Matt coolly.

" Den give us one now."

" You will have to wait until I am done tuning up, gentlemen."

" All right, we'll wait."

Matt tuned up more slowly than ever, and even allowed one of the strings to break that he might gain an extra minute in repairing the damage. At ·

last, after fully five minutes had passed, the banjo
was in order for use, and the young auctioneer
struck off a few chords.

" Now give us dat jig if yo' kin play it," said the
colored man impatiently. He was the same who
had tried to steal the box of chains.

" I won't play a jig until you and your companion pay for the glass you broke," returned Matt
shortly, and he laid down the instrument abruptly,
and folded his arms.

" Wot ?" roared the colored men in concert.

" You heard what I said."

" See here; do yo' want us to smash de hull
place ?" demanded the ringleader of the disturbers.

" I don't think you'll smash anything more,"
replied Matt.

" I won't, hey ?   We'll see !"

The colored man made a movement as if to strike
the young auctioneer in the face. But before the
blow could land he was hauled back by a strong
arm. He and his companions looked around and
found themselves confronted by two policemen
whom Andy had fortunately met upon the corner
below.

The two colored men who had kept somewhat in
the background at once sneaked through the crowd

and escaped through the open doorway. The other two, the ones who had done the damage, were held by the policemen, much to their discomfiture.

A lively talk followed, and then upon payment for the damage done, the colored men were allowed to go, first being warned by Matt and Andy not to show themselves in the store again. Had they not paid up they would have been arrested.

After this scene was ended one of the policemen remained in the vicinity of the place for all the while the store remained open. But nothing more occurred to disturb the auction sales.

Business in Easton was so good that they remained there until Tuesday of the following week. During that time they took in nearly two hundred dollars, leaving them a profit, after all expenses were met, of forty-five dollars.

On Saturday morning Matt and Andy were called to Belvidere, the county seat, to testify against Barberry for the robbery at Phillipsburg. Strange to say, Barberry pleaded guilty, so the two boys had no trouble in the way of being detained as witnesses against him. The corn salve doctor was held for sentence.

After leaving Easton Matt and Andy struck out for Bethlehem and Allentown. The weather was now growing gradually colder, but they calculated that they would have at least a month of weather which would be fit to travel in, even in this mountainous country.

"At Allentown we can stop long enough for me to take a trip to Philadelphia and buy goods," remarked Andy as they were driving out of Easton.

"Just as you say," returned Matt. "I am glad we have to stock up so often, and I am looking forward to the time when it will be necessary for us to buy a larger wagon and get another horse to put beside Billy."

"It will hardly pay us to buy another horse this fall. You must remember that we are to locate in some place during the winter. I have no desire to move around much when the thermometer is below the freezing point."

They were soon on the outskirts of Easton, and then they struck a rather rough road leading over numerous hills and around jagged rocks.

"By jinks! I believe we have missed the way," remarked Matt, as at last he brought Billy to a standstill. "That stable-keeper said the road was a good one, and I fail to find this so."

"We'll stop at the next house and find out," returned Andy. "Do you see any place in sight?"

"There is a cottage down in the hollow yonder. Stay here with Billy, and I'll ask the way there."

Matt sprang from the wagon and was soon hurrying across a barren bit of pasture land that led down to a brook which was all but dried up. The cottage stood upon the bank of the brook, and walking up to it, the young auctioneer rapped upon the door.

There was an exclamation of surprise from within, and then he was asked to enter. He did so, and was greatly vexed to find himself in the presence of three of the colored men who had created the disturbance in the store but a few nights before!

CHAPTER XXX.

A DASH FROM DANGER.

HAD Matt known that he would meet three of the colored men in the cottage in the hollow, it is more than likely that he would not have gone near the place.

When he and Andy had had the trouble at the store, the two men who had been compelled to pay for the broken glass had gone off in anything but a happy frame of mind, and the young auctioneer had then remarked to his partner that they might have trouble with the men should they chance to meet them away from police protection.

Matt saw at once that the negroes recognized him, and that his reception would be far from agreeable. Had he been less courageous he would have turned and fled, but as it was, he stood his ground.

All three of the colored men had been seated around a kitchen table playing cards, but at his

entrance the two who had been the primary cause
of the former trouble sprang to their feet and came
toward him.

"Huh! what brings yo' heah?" demanded the
ringleader of the mischief-makers wrathfully.

For the instant Matt hardly knew how to reply.
He recognized his mistake in coming to the cottage,
and he was anxious now to make as early a departure as possible.

"Do you live here?" he asked boldly.

"Yes we do," returned the colored man.

"Then I have made a mistake in coming here.   I
thought some one else might live here."

And he took a step backward to the door.

"Hol' on!" exclaimed the colored man, coming
still closer.   "What brung yo' heah?"

"I wanted to find out if we were on the right
road, that was all.   But I can find out elsewhere."

"Whar's yo' wagon?"

"Over on the road," and Matt waved his hand in
the direction.

"Gwine to leave Easton?" questioned the second
colored man.

"Yes."

No sooner had Matt made the reply than the three
colored men glanced at each other, and the ringleader whispered to his companions.

"See yeah, yo' ain't gwine befo' we is squar' wid yo'!" he cried, as he caught Matt by the arm.

"Let go of me!" exclaimed the young auctioneer. "I won't stand being molested!"

"We'll see about dat!" cried the second colored man, and he also caught hold of Matt.

"Close dat doah, Shelby!" went on the ringleader, to the man still at the table. "Dis is just de chance we wanted at dis yeah boy!"

The man addressed at once arose, and rushing to the somewhat rickety door, not only closed it, but also locked it.

Matt viewed this movement with increased alarm, and squirmed to release himself, but without avail.

"Yo' can't git away from us, nohow!" cried the ringleader, as he squeezed the young auctioneer's arm until Matt thought he would crack a bone. "We is gwine for to teach you a lesson, boy, dat yo' won't forgit in a long while!"

"Help! help!" yelled Matt, without more ado, realizing that the situation was becoming suddenly desperate.

He had barely time to repeat his cry when the ringleader of the negroes clapped his big hand over his mouth. Then he was forced over backward upon the floor.

" Go frough his pockets, Jeff !"

" Dat's wot I intends to do, Tooker!"

" He's got a putty good watch."

" Maybe he's got a lot o' money, too."

The rascals began to go through Matt's pockets, and he called Jeff made a movement toward relieving the boy of his watch and chain.

The timepiece had once belonged to Mr. Lincoln, and to the young auctioneer it was a valuable heirloom. The thought that he was to be deprived of it angered him more than did anything else, and he began to kick out hotly right and left.

The negroes were not prepared for this, and before they could guard against it, one received a severe blow in the chin, and the other had the toe of Matt's shoe nearly knock out his eye. They both gave sharp cries of pain and fell back, and taking advantage of this Matt leaped to his feet.

" Open that!" he commanded, to the third negro, who stood with his back against the door. " Open that before I make it warm for you also!"

But the colored man would not budge, and Matt was compelled to attack him in his fight for freedom.

The young auctioneer was thoroughly aroused, and now showed what muscle he had gained during his free-and-easy life on the road. He attacked the man without hesitation, and forcing him aside, compelled him to keep away from the door by blows and kicks delivered with surprising rapidity.

The man had, at the last moment, taken the key from the lock and thrown it in the far corner of the room. Not waiting to recover this, Matt began to hammer at the door, and gathering himself together, threw his whole weight against it.

As has been said, the door was a rickety one, and it went down with a crash, tumbling the young auctioneer upon his face just outside the cottage.

"Hullo! what on earth does this mean?" cried a voice close by, and Andy rushed up, a look of blank astonishment plainly depicted upon his face.

"Those negroes!" gasped Matt, struggling to rise from amid the wreckage of the door. "Come on, don't wait, for they are three to two, and they are just drunk enough to be as ugly as sin!"

He caught Andy by the arm, and before the latter could ask for a further explanation, hurried him up the hill toward the wagon.

The negroes came out of the cottage and made after them, but only for a short distance. Then they came to a sudden halt, and after a brief consultation, hurried back to the cottage.

"What do you suppose they went back for—pistols and razors?" questioned Andy, as they reached

the turn-out, and he unhitched Billy from the tree
to which he had been tied.

"No, they are afraid we are going after the
police," returned Matt, springing up to the seat.
"Every one of that crowd ought to be in jail this
minute!" he went on bitterly.

"What did they do to you?"

"Nearly robbed me!" And in a few brief words
he related what had happened to him.

"Well, do you want to go back to Easton and
make a complaint?" asked Andy, when he had finished.

"No, I am sick of having to do with the police,
Andy. All I want is to be let alone."

"That's my sentiment, Matt. We are out for
business—and money—not trouble."

Andy sprang up beside Matt, and it was soon decided by the partners to continue on the road until
another house should appear. They looked back,
but saw nothing more of the negroes, and then
started off.

They passed through a bit of woods and down a
long hill. Here they found a neat farmhouse, where
a pleasant enough woman was sitting upon the door-
step, knitting socks.

"This is one road, but it is not the best road,"
replied the woman, in reply to Andy's question

regarding the way to Bethlehem. "But now you are this far, you had better keep on, for it will be harder to turn back."

"How far is it to the town?"

"Not over a mile and a half."

"And is the road fairly good from here?"

"Oh, yes; you can get along very well."

"Then we will continue," returned Andy. "By the way," he went on, "do you know anything of the negroes that live in the cottage back a ways?"

The woman's face lost its smile and she sighed.

"Yes, I know them only too well," she replied. "They have stolen so many of our chickens and so much garden truck that my husband is going to make a complaint against them. I wish they would leave the neighborhood."

"I trust your husband succeeds in having them all locked up," put in Matt, "for they richly deserve it." And after a few words more with the farmer's wife they passed on.

It was getting on toward noon when they finally arrived at Bethlehem, that pretty little town on the Lehigh River. They drove past several of the silk mills, and finally found a livery stable, at which Billy and the wagon were put up.

"It looks as if we might do some business here,"

said Andy, as they started for a restaurant for dinner. " Let us open up this afternoon if possible."

"Shall we hire a store?"

" Let us try to sell from the wagon first."

Immediately after dinner they procured a license and found a suitable corner. They did all in their power to attract a crowd, and finally, toward evening, when the working people were on their way home, succeeded in bringing quite an assemblage around them.

But, strange to say, they could not make a single sale, try their best. Both used up all their eloquence; Matt played on the banjo and mouth harmonica, and Andy told funny stories. It was no use; the crowd merely smiled or frowned, and then one after another drifted away.

" This is the worst luck yet," whispered Andy to Matt. " I never dreamed that we would strike anything like this."

A stout German who stood in the crowd saw the look of wonder and disappointment on Andy's face, and he laughed heartily.

" You ton't vos caught der same pirds twice alretty!" he chuckled to several bystanders.

" What's that?" questioned Matt, who overheard the remark.

" You ton't vos caught der same pirds twice mit

der same salt," returned the German, and he laughed heartily at what he considered a good joke, while those around smiled and nodded approvingly.

"I must say I don't see the joke," said Matt cheerfully. "Won't you let me in the secret?"

"Dose udder fellers vos schwindle us, put you can't do it twice times!" was the reply.

"Other fellows swindled you?" repeated Matt.

"Yes, dose fellers mit dot wagon vot vas here all last week. I don't dink but vot you vos der same crowd of fellers!"

CHAPTER XXXI.

DANGEROUS MOUNTAIN TRAVELING.

Both Matt and Andy began to smell a mouse, as the saying is, and they lost no time in questioning not only the German, but several other people that remained around the wagon.

The young auctioneers soon learned that a rival party of auctioneers with a large two-horse wagon had stopped at the town during the entire previous week, and sold goods which were next to worthless, for the highest prices to be obtained. They had been cool and shrewd men, thoroughly dishonest, and they had swindled every one who had had dealings with them.

"And where did they go to?" asked Andy, of the German, after the matter had been talked over for some time.

"Ve ton't know. Of ve did ve vould tar an' fedder dem, py chiminy!" was the emphatic reply.

"That settles it, we won't be able to do any business here," said Matt, and though they remained in

Bethlehem the remainder of that day and all of the next, his words proved true. Only a few trifles were sold, and these at prices that did not reimburse them for the trouble of handling.

Seeing that it would not pay to remain in the town longer, they started once more on the road, and by the end of the week found themselves established in a store in Allentown, and doing quite a good business.

While in this city Andy made a trip to Philadelphia, and had several more cases of goods shipped on, which Matt was careful to procure before they might be stolen from the freight depot. The wagon was also sent to a repair shop and thoroughly overhauled, for the roads beyond Allentown promised to be rougher than those heretofore traversed.

Both Matt and Andy were curious to know more about the rival auctioneers, and they wondered if they would meet the men. Nothing had been heard of them in Allentown, so that their business in that city was not injured. They did fairly well, although a strike in some of the mills made business duller than it would otherwise have been.

But both of the partners thought they had no cause for complaint. During the time they had been away from home they had cleared, above all expenses, one hundred and seventy-two dollars, which, equally divided, was eighty-six dollars apiece—not a fortune, but still an amount which Matt at least viewed with considerable satisfaction.

"If we do as well right straight through," he said, as he and Andy talked it over on their way to Lehighton and Mauch Chunk, "we will have quite an amount to place to our credit in the bank by the time we reach New York again."

"I am in hopes that we will do even better as cold weather comes on," returned Andy. "Folks seem to buy more then—I don't know why. And besides, after stopping at Mauch Chunk, we will only go to large places, for I think it will pay to skip the smaller ones."

"I don't know but what you are right. I know one thing that I am going to do when I get to Mauch Chunk—that is, if business continues good."

"And what is that?"

"I am going to buy a post-office order and send Miss Bartlett the money she so kindly loaned me. Won't she be surprised to get it back so soon?"

"No doubt of it, Matt. It was very kind of her to loan it to you. I suppose you are going to pay her the interest——"

"For the full year," finished the boy. "And at Christmas, if I can do it, I'm going to make her some sort of a nice present. She is the only friend I had left in New York."

"A very nice young lady," returned Andy, and then he went on, with a short laugh: "I wonder what old Caleb Gulligan would say if he knew of our prosperity?"

"And I wonder what Mr. Randolph Fenton would say if he knew how I was doing? I hope when I write to Miss Bartlett that she lets him know," went on Matt. "I suppose he thought that after he discharged me I would go to the dogs."

"Yes, men like him very often imagine the world cannot possibly get along without them. I reckon you are glad that you are no longer in his employ."

"Glad isn't a strong enough word, Andy. It makes me shudder to look back at the times I spent in his offices, being bossed around and scolded from morning to night."

"I think traveling around has done us both a deal of good, Matt. I feel stronger than I have in years, and you look the picture of health, barring those bruises you received from Barberry and his companions."

"Oh, I feel fine! Outdoor life always did agree with me. When I was in Fenton's offices I felt very much like a prisoner in a jail. I wouldn't go back to that life again for the world!"

Thus the talk ran on, from one subject to another. Andy had given his young partner the full particulars of his own roving life, and in return Matt had related everything concerning himself, and the two felt as if they had known each other for years; in fact, as Matt once stated later on, they were more like brothers than mere partners in business.

Andy was deeply interested in the fact of Mr. Lincoln's disappearance, and he wondered nearly as much as did Matt himself if the unfortunate man would ever turn up again.

As for the boy, he could not bring himself to believe that his parent was dead, and although he rarely mentioned his father's name, he was constantly on the watch for him, and often when they were stopping at a place he would go off on what he termed a " still hunt," hoping thereby to pick up a stray bit of information which would put him on the right track to learn of his father's whereabouts.

The drive up through Walnut Port to Lehigh Gap was very nice. At the latter place they stopped over night, and then pushed on to Lehighton, sometimes along the river, and then by way of a road through and around the mountains.

" This scenery is just grand!" cried Matt, as they were driving on about ten o'clock in the forenoon.

"Just look at that mountain over yonder! And see how the river winds along through the valley below here!"

"It is very fine, indeed!" returned Andy. "But I'll tell you what: I would rather be on horseback than in the wagon. It seems to me that some of the bends around the mountain side are positively dangerous."

"Oh, I guess not, Andy. Why, look, there is a regular wagon road. If other wagons can pass along here, I fancy we can do so, too."

"Other wagons may not be as heavy as ours, with that big case tied on behind. Don't you notice how Billy slips every once in awhile?"

"Well, we might have had him shod sharp when we had the wagon overhauled," returned Matt slowly, as he noticed for the first time that Billy did slip more than usual. "We can have it done during our stop at Mauch Chunk or at Lehighton, if it becomes necessary. Maybe we are on the wrong road again."

"Well, certainly this road is growing worse instead of better," said Andy soberly. "Just look at that turn ahead! The road isn't over ten feet wide, and it slopes down to that steep hill——"

"Drive as close to the inside wall as you can," was Matt's somewhat nervous reply, as he saw the possible danger ahead. "Steady now, Billy, steady!"

The horse moved along slowly up to the curve which ran around the mountain side. As Andy had said, the road at this point was scarcely ten feet wide, and on the other side was a steep downward slope, terminating below at a tiny brook filled with loose rocks.

The curve was reached, and the two were just congratulating themselves upon having passed the dangerous spot in safety, when a large bird, flying from a near-by bush, frightened Billy and caused him to shy to one side.

In another instant the wagon was at the very edge of the slope!

CHAPTER XXXII.

AN INTERESTING LETTER.

To Andy and Matt it looked as if the entire turn-out must slide down the hillside to the bottom, there to be smashed into a hundred pieces.

It was small wonder, therefore, that both gave a loud cry of alarm and that both caught at the lines to lead Billy away from the danger so imminent.

The horse continued to move ahead, but instead of drawing closer to the inside, he walked upon the very outer edge of the road.

"I'll lead him!" cried Andy, and while Matt continued to hold the lines, he sprang out and caught Billy by the bridle.

Ordinarily, the faithful animal would have come along willingly, but he now seemed to grow obstinate, and pulled back when Andy caught hold. The wagon stopped, and then the rear wheels were sent partly down the slope.

"Pull him up!" cried Matt. "Pull him, Andy!"

" He won't come!" gasped Andy, tugging at the bridle with might and main.

"But he must come! The wagon will go down in another second!"

" I can't help it, I can't make him come," panted Andy, between his clinched teeth, as he renewed the struggle to bring the wagon up on the level once more.

Tying the lines fast, Matt sprang out. He had seen a loose stone of fair size close at hand, and this he now picked up. Running around to the rear of the wagon, he placed it on the sloping ground so that one of the wheels was blocked from further slipping.

" Good!" cried Andy. "Can you find another stone?"

" I'm going to push on the other wheel. Get up, Billy, get up there!"

Matt placed his shoulder to the wheel, and exerted all of his strength, and seeing this, Andy also urged the horse. Billy gave a tug—there was a moment's strain—and then the turn-out rolled up once more upon the level road.

"Thank goodness for that!" burst out Andy. " I thought for a moment that it was a goner!"

" So did I, Andy. You had better lead him until we reach a safer bit of the road."

"I intend to do that. And after this I'll know enough to lead him around such a bend, instead of taking such a dangerous chance."

Only a hundred feet further on the mountain road left the proximity of the slope, and then the two once more climbed up on the seat. Billy, the horse, did not appear to be in the least disturbed over the adventure, but Matt and Andy were bathed in a cold perspiration which did not leave them until some time after.

At Lehighton, where they stopped for dinner, they determined to drive right through to Mauch Chunk, four miles further on. Many people from the former place did their trading at Mauch Chunk, and the young auctioneers thought they would catch just as much trade by not stopping on the way.

At Mauch Chunk a stop was made for three days, and during that time there were several excursions to the place from New York and Philadelphia, the city folks coming up to see the autumnal beauties of Glen Onoko and the various mountains through which the Switchback gravity road runs. These crowds helped business some, and the stay proved nearly as profitable as the one at Easton had been.

On the first day at Mauch Chunk Matt procured the money order of which he had spoken, and sent it to Ida Bartlett, with a long letter, in which he thanked her for her kindness, and gave her an account of the trip since leaving the metropolis. He stated that if she wished to write to him within the week to address the letter to Wilkesbarre, or, on the following week to Scranton, as they were bound for both places.

During their spare hours both Andy and Matt took the ride on the gravity road and enjoyed it very much. The rhododendrons were out in full bloom, and Matt wished he could send Ida Bartlett · a bunch of the beautiful flowers.

They were soon once again on the road. But Billy's shoes had been carefully attended to, and now they were very careful whenever they came to a spot that looked at all dangerous.

" One scare is enough," was the way Andy put it, and Matt thoroughly agreed with him.

After leaving Mauch Chunk they passed through Penn Haven and Leslie Run, and so on to White Haven. At the latter place they stopped for two days, but found it very unprofitable, as there was little or no money afloat.

" Well, we have to take the bad with the good," said Andy, in reply to Matt's remark concerning the dullness of trade. " We cannot expect to make money wherever we go. If that was to be done, I reckon there would be many other auctioneers in the field."

" That reminds me : I wonder what has become of those auctioneers we heard of in Bethlehem?"

" I'm sure I don't know. But it is likely that we will hear from them again, sooner or later."

On leaving White Haven for Wilkesbarre, they struck the first snow-storm of the season. It was not a heavy storm, and yet, as the wind blew in their faces, the drive of thirty miles proved anything but pleasant. They were glad enough when the city was reached, and they were able to put up the turn-out at a livery stable and warm up around the office stove.

" We won't be able to travel much longer, if this keeps on," remarked Andy. " We'll have to pick out some place to settle down in for the winter."

" Have you any place in view?" asked Matt, with interest.

" I've had my eye on Middletown, New York State. That's a lively place, and it gets a trade from a good many miles around."

" Do you think we can make it ?"

" I think so. We can go from Scranton to Carbondale, and Honesdale, and so on through Lackawaxen and Port Jervis. By taking that route we can stop on the way and still reach Middletown inside of two weeks."

" Well. I shouldn't like to miss a letter from Miss Bartlett, if it was sent."

" You can leave directions to forward it if it comes after we are gone.   The post-office authorities will willingly send the letter wherever you direct."

" Perhaps she has already written."

" If you think so, why don't you call at the post-office and find out ?"

" I will—as soon as we have had something to eat and drink."

They passed over to the Commercial Hotel, and after brushing up, entered the dining-room.   Here a late dinner was served for them, and it is needless to say that both did full justice to all that was set before them.

After they had finished Andy went off to hunt up an empty store, and Matt, after securing directions, walked off to the post-office.

To his delight, there was a letter for him, and addressed in Ida Bartlett's hand.   As it was the first letter he had received since being on the road, the reader can understand his curiosity to master its contents.   Standing back in an out-of-the-way spot of the corridor, he split open the envelope with his penknife, and was soon reading that which had been written.

The letter surprised him not a little. After acknowledging the receipt of the money order and congratulating him upon his evident success, Ida Bartlett wrote as follows:

" And now, Matt, I am going to tell you something that I think will interest you even more than it does me. It is about Mr. Fenton and the mining shares which he once sold your father. Last week Mr. Gaston, the bookkeeper, had a quarrel with Mr. Fenton, and was discharged. Before he left, however, he and Mr. Fenton had some high words, which I, being in the next office, could not help hearing.

" During this quarrel something was said about the shares sold to William Lincoln, and Mr. Gaston said that if the papers in connection with the shares which your father had bought could be recovered, he would expose Mr. Fenton. I could not understand the whole drift of the matter, but Mr. Fenton seemed to be glad that your father was missing—he said he was most likely dead—and that the papers had disappeared with him.

" Do you know anything of the papers? Mr. Gaston has gone to Boston, but I could write to him if you think that Mr. Fenton is a swindler and that you can get back any money which he may have defrauded your father out of. I myself am going to leave Mr. Fenton's employ on the first of next month, having secured a better place with another firm of brokers. Let me hear from you again as soon as possible. I hope if he has any money belonging to your father you can get it."

CHAPTER XXXIII.

THE RIVAL AUCTIONEERS.

It may well be imagined that Matt read Ida Bartlett's letter with great interest. The young auctioneer had never received a communication as surprising as was this one.

He went over every word carefully several times, then placed the letter in his pocket, and started off to find Andy.

Half an hour later he came across his partner on the main street. Andy had just rented a store, one of two vacant ones which were side by side, and was now on his way to drive the wagon around and unload the stock.

" Well, did you get a letter, Matt ?"

" I did."

" Good enough. Any special news ?"

" Yes, indeed. Just read that."

And the young auctioneer passed the communication over for his partner's perusal,

Andy read the letter as carefully as had Matt. He emitted a long, low whistle.

" What do you think of it?"

" I hardly know what to think, Matt. Do you know anything about this mining share business?"

" I know that Randolph Fenton sold my father some shares, that is all. I never saw the certificates, if that is what they are called."

" Did you ever see the papers in connection with the shares?"

" No."

" Then they must have been in your father's possession when he disappeared."

" I don't know about that. Mother might have had them when father was first sent to the asylum for treatment. Although I remember hearing her once say that since father's mind had become affected he would not trust any one with his affairs, but kept all his money and papers hidden away."

" It's too bad you haven't the papers."

" That's so. If I had them I would hunt up Mr. Gaston, and get him to expose Randolph Fenton."

" It might pay you to do that anyway."

" I don't know. If there was any likelihood of this being the case, I think Miss Bartlett would have written to that effect."

" What do you intend to do?"

"I am going to write to her again, telling her just how matters stand with me, and ask her if she thinks it will do any good for me to come on. If she thinks it will, I'll try to manage it some way to take a run to New York."

"You can do that whenever you wish, Matt. I will take care of things the same as you did when I was gone."

On the way to the stable where the wagon and Billy were located they talked the matter over at a greater length. Andy took a warm personal interest in the matter, and did not hesitate to say so.

"If this Fenton swindled your father, I trust you are able to prove it and get your money back," he said. "I don't know of any one that deserves money more than you do."

The wagon was soon driven around to the store, and the goods unloaded. Then the show-window and the shelves were arranged to attract the eye, after which Andy hung out the red flag, which now began to look to the young auctioneers like an old friend.

As soon as everything was in shape for business Matt brought out paper, pen and ink, and set to work upon the letter to Ida Bartlett. At first he hardly knew how to express himself, but before he had finished he had filled eight pages, and told the young lady exactly how matters stood. He begged for her further assistance, and assured her that she should not lose through her kindness to him.

The letter finished, Matt did not place it in a letter-box, but marched with it to the post-office, that it might be included with the first out-going New York mail.

"If I only could find father," he sighed to himself as he turned back to the store. "Something in my heart tells me that he is not dead, and yet, if this is so, where can he be?"

On arriving at the store he found Andy already busy with a crowd which had begun to collect the moment that the red flag was hung out. Matt had to begin work at once, and this was a good thing for the boy, for it kept him from brooding over his parent's possible fate and thus growing melancholy.

"If I am any kind of a judge, we are going to do the best business yet at this city," said Andy, as there came a little lull in trade. "It started off briskly, and it has kept on steadily ever since."

"Well, that just suits me," laughed Matt. "To my way of thinking we cannot do too much business."

During the next day Matt noticed two sharp-eyed men hanging around the place a good deal.

At first he paid no attention to them, but at last pointed them out to Andy.

"Yes, I noticed them myself," returned the senior partner. "They do not look as if they wanted to buy, but just as if they were spying."

"Supposing I call them in and ask them to buy?" suggested Matt, for both of the men were at that moment gazing in the window at the articles displayed there.

"Certainly, you can do that if you want to," returned Andy.

So Matt walked from behind the counter toward the door, but before he could reach it one of the men saw him and spoke to his companion, and both hurried up the street and around the nearest corner.

"Humph! that's queer, to say the least," said the young auctioneer, and Andy agreed with him.

There had been a "To Let" bill upon the show-window of the vacant store next door, but on the following morning when the young auctioneers opened up they found the bill gone. The door of the store was open, and inside a boy somewhat younger than Matt was cleaning up.

"Hullo!" cried Matt, stopping short. Then he poked his head in at the door and confronted the boy.

"So we are going to have neighbors, eh?" he remarked pleasantly.

"Bet your life!" was the slangy reply from the boy, as soon as he had noted who had addressed him. "You didn't expect us, did you?"

"No, I didn't know the store was taken until a moment ago," said Matt.

"Well, it can't be helped. It was the only store vacant in the neighborhood."

"Can't be helped?" repeated Matt, somewhat puzzled. "What do you mean?"

"Oh, I thought you might object to our opening up alongside of you."

"I don't see why I should. What business are you in?"

"Same line."

Matt was taken aback somewhat by this unexpected reply, and his face showed it.

"Do you mean to say you are going to open an auction store here?"

"That's it, and we are going to make it everlastingly warm for you fellows, too," went on the boy triumphantly. "We've been a-watching how you run things, and we are going to scoop every bit of trade when we get started."

Matt drew a long breath. Here was certainly a new experience. He and Andy had expected to encounter rivals, but had never dreamed of having them at such close quarters.

"Well, I suppose we will have to stand it," he said, hardly knowing how else to reply to the boy's bragging statement.

"If I was you I'd pack up and try some other place," went on the boy. "Gissem & Fillow will take every bit of trade—they always do wherever they go."

"Gissem & Fillow? Are those the names of the men who run the concern?"

"Yes, and they are the slickest auctioneers in the country."

"Perhaps you only think so."

"Oh, I know it. I'll bet you a new hat you don't take in a dollar after we get a-going."

"Thank you, but I don't bet. May I ask where you came from?"

"We came from Stroudsburg."

"Were you down in Bethlehem before that?"

"Yes. How did you know that?"

"We came through there after you had gone."

"Bet you didn't sell anything. We squeezed the town dry."

"We didn't sell much," returned Matt. He was on the point of stating that he had heard how the folks had been swindled, but he changed his mind. "How long do you expect to remain here?"

"Oh, a week or so. You might as well pack up and leave."

"I guess we will venture to remain, at least a day or two longer," said Matt. "Perhaps we'll be able to do a little in spite of you."

At that moment a large wagon began to back up to the curb. The seat was occupied by two men, and Matt at once recognized them as the fellows he had caught hanging around the previous day. They were the rival auctioneers, who had been watching to learn how Matt and Andy conducted their business.

CHAPTER XXXIV.

MATT SPEAKS HIS MIND.

MATT did not wait to encounter the rival auction-eers, but walked away and entered the door of his own store. Andy was busy, dusting up, and to his partner he told what he had heard.

"Phew!" whistled Andy. "That will make mat-ters rather interesting. Is that their wagon out there?"

"I suppose it is. Those are the same two men, I am certain."

"Yes, they are. Well, if they are the swindlers folks in Bethlehem said they were we ought not to fear them. People are not fools, and they soon learn if a man is honest or not."

"They may take away a good bit of trade, never-theless, Andy. And we were just congratulating ourselves on what a fine week we were going to have."

"We must do our best, Matt. This puts me on my mettle."

They talked the matter over a bit, and then set to work to "put their best foot forward," as Andy termed it. The window was cleaned as it had never been cleaned before, and also the show-cases and shelves, and then they proceeded to make the most elaborate display possible.

"There; that ought to attract people, if anything will," remarked Andy, when the work was finished.

"You are right; the window couldn't look better. But perhaps they will put out big price signs."

"Never mind, they can't afford to sell any cheaper than we can. I bought all the goods at bottom figures. Let us start up before they get ready."

They began to play on several instruments, and as soon as half a dozen people were collected Andy began to talk and tell jokes. Before the rival auctioneers had their stock inside of their store Matt and Andy were doing a pretty fair business.

Seeing this, Gissem & Fillow hurried up their preparations, and by noon both places were "going it for all they were worth," as Matt expressed it.

Gissem seemed to be the principal member of the firm, Fillow and the boy being merely helpers. He was a tall, thin-faced and clean-shaven man, with hard, steely-blue eyes.

"This way for bargains!" he cried out, coming out upon the sidewalk. "This way, gents and

ladies! The only place in Wilkesbarre selling reli-
able goods at rock-bottom figures! Don't be de-
ceived by rival concerns trying to obtain a bit of
our well-earned prosperity! Come right in and be
convinced!" And he kept on in this strain for fully
five minutes.

"Well, that is what I call downright mean," cried
Matt to Andy. "Of course all these cracks at rival
concerns are meant for us. He wants to draw the
crowd away from us."

"More than that, he is trying to scare them, so
that if they won't patronize him they won't purchase anywhere," returned the senior partner. "It
is certainly not a fair way to do."

"Can't we stop, him, Andy?"

"I don't see how. He has mentioned no names."

Andy began to talk, but as he was inside of the
store while Gissem was outside, very few of the
people on the street were attracted. They made
several sales to those inside, but after the purchasers
were gone the store was empty. In the meantime,
the next place was filled to overflowing.

"Let us give them a tune," suggested Matt. "I
see our rivals have no musical instruments."

He brought out a banjo, and Andy took up the
largest accordion in the place. Sitting down in a

spot from which the music could float out of the door, they played several of their best selections.

The music pleased many people. They stopped listening to Gissem, and after some hesitation several came in. More followed, and seeing this, Matt and Andy kept on until the store was once more filled.

Then Matt began to talk. He made no wild statements, but in an earnest manner told what they had to sell, and asked those around him to examine the goods carefully.

"That fellow next door said to beware of rival concerns," remarked a man in the crowd slyly, and several smiled at the words.

"Well, I take it that people are bright enough to know what they are doing," returned Matt. "We are too busy to talk about our neighbors. We are here to show what we have and sell goods—if we can. We do not misrepresent, and if any one is dissatisfied with his purchase he can return it and get his money back. Isn't that fair enough?"

"I reckon it is."

"We carry a large stock, as you can see, and we sell everything for what it is."

"Let me see those spoons, will you?" questioned a man standing beside the one talking to Matt.

"Certainly, sir," and the young auctioneer handed over several samples.

" Are these triple plated ?"

" No, sir; they are single plated, on white metal."

" Then they are just as good as triple plated ?"

" Almost as good, for ordinary wear. Here are some that are triple plated."

" I know they are."

" Oh, you do."

" Yes, I know all about spoons, for I used to be in the plating business. I only asked to see what you would say. That man next door tried to sell my friend some single plated ones for triple plated. I brought him in here to see what you had to say about your stock."

" Well, I have not misrepresented, have I ?"

" No; you have told the exact truth. John, if you want any spoons, you might as well buy them here, for I see they are put at a very reasonable figure."

Upon this, the man who had first spoken began to pick out some of the goods. What his friend had said had been heard by the crowd, who now began to feel more like trusting in what the young auctioneers might have to say.

Matt sold the spoons, and in the meantime Andy put up a number of other articles at auction, and **sold them at fairly good prices.**

They managed to keep busy until two o'clock in the afternoon, when trade fell off once more. Seeing this, Andy prepared to go out to dinner. He had just put on his hat when Gissem, the rival auctioneer, rushed in.

"See here, I want to talk to you two fellows!" he blustered.

"Well, what is it?" questioned Matt, as coolly as he could.

"You've been telling people I tried to stick a man on a lot of tin-plated spoons, saying they were solid silver."

"Who said so?"

"Never mind who said so. Let me tell you I ain't going to stand such work."

"Excuse me, sir, but we circulated no such story," interrupted Andy. "We know enough to mind our own business."

"But they told me one or the other of you had said so. We won't stand that—we'll have you arrested for—for defamation of character!" stormed the rival auctioneer, working himself up into a fine pitch of assumed indignation.

"We have said nothing concerning you," said Matt. "We have not even advised people to beware of our rivals, nor have we mentioned your stop in Bethlehem, and how the folks of that town regarded your doings there," he went on pointedly.

" What—what do you mean?" stammered Gissem, taken by surprise.

" I mean just what I infer. We know how people there were swindled, and we know how anxious some of them are to lay hands on a certain firm of auctioneers."

" Have a care, boy, or I'll—I'll——"

" What will you do?"

" Never mind; you'll see fast enough."

" You cannot bully me. Now that you have taken the trouble to come in here, let me tell you something. You just cast several reflections upon our characters. That has got to be stopped."

" Humph! Why, you are but a boy and dare talk to me."

" Never mind, he knows what he is saying," put in Andy. " We are not to be mistreated by rivals or by any one else."

" Don't talk to me!" snapped Gissem, and unable to keep up the talk with credit to himself, he fled from the store.

" I don't think he will dare to bother us again," said Andy. " He is too much afraid to have his past record raked up."

Andy went off to dinner, leaving Matt in sole

charge. The snow had cleared away, but it was still cold, and to keep himself warm, Matt went to the rear of the establishment and got his overcoat. He was just putting on the garment when a noise near the show-window attracted his attention. He ran forward, and saw that a thin stream of water was coming down through the boards of the ceiling. The water was splashing on some of the stock, and unless it was speedily checked it would do a good bit of damage.

Matt knew that the upper part of the building was not occupied. In the rear of the store was a door leading to the back hallway, and through this he ran and started to go upstairs.

As he did so, somebody started to come down. It was the boy who worked for the rival auctioneers.

CHAPTER XXXV.

TOM IN WOLD.

As soon as the boy saw Matt he stopped short, and then endeavored to retreat. But Matt was coming up the steps in a tremendous hurry, and in ten seconds he was close enough to the boy to catch him by the arm.

"Let go of me!" cried the boy, badly frightened.

"What have you done?" questioned Matt sternly, and without waiting for a reply, forced the boy to accompany him into the rooms.

A glance around revealed the cause of the flood below. In one of the rooms was a sink with city water. The water had been turned on full, and the sink-holes stopped up with putty. The sink had overflowed, and the water was running through several cracks in the floor.

As rapidly as he could Matt turned off the faucet. Then leaving the water still in the sink to the brim, he dashed downstairs.

"You come with me and help me save my stock!"

he cried to the boy. " If you don't I'll hand you over to the first policeman I can find."

" Oh, please don't have me arrested !" howled the boy, almost scared out of his wits by the threat. " I—I—didn't mean any harm !"

" You didn't mean any harm? We'll see. Come down now."

The boy hesitated, and then followed Matt into the store. Here a portion of the stock had to be removed, and then the young auctioneer set the boy to work mopping up the water on the counter and the floor.

" Say, please don't have me arrested, will you ?" asked the boy, almost in tears over what he considered a very serious predicament.

" You ought to be taught a lesson," returned Matt severely. " What put you up to the idea of letting the water overflow ?"

" What Mr. Gissem said. He was awful mad after he was in here, and he told Mr. Fillow he wished that you would burn out or that the water pipes would burst and drown you out. Then he asked me if I couldn't worry you a bit, and I said I'd try, and that's the truth of it."

" Well, that man ought to be cowhided !" was Matt's vigorous exclamation. " Excuse me, but is he any relation to you ?"

" Oh, no."

" Is Mr. Fillow ?"

" No, neither of them."

" Then how do you come to be traveling with them ?"

The boy's face took on a sober look, and he swallowed something like a lump in his throat.

" I—I got tired of going to school and I ran away from home."

" What do you mean—" Matt stopped short as a certain thought flashed over his mind. " Say, is your name Tom Inwold, and do you come from Plainfield ?"

At this unexpected question the boy looked at Matt in amazement, his mouth wide open, and his eyes as big as they could well be.

" Who told you who I was ?" he gasped.

" No one ; I guessed it."

" But I don't know you."

" That's true. We stopped in Plainfield a number of weeks ago, and there I met your mother."

" And what did she say ?" faltered Tom Inwold.

" She told me that you had run away with an auctioneer."

" And—and was that all ?" went on the boy, his voice trembling with emotion.

" No ; she was very anxious to have you come

home again. She missed you very much, and she
could not understand how you could have the heart
to leave her."

At these words, which Matt delivered very
seriously, the tears sprang into Tom Inwold's eyes.
Evidently he was not hard-hearted, and had been
led astray purely by bad associates.

"I—I wish I was back home again," he said in a
low voice.

"You do not like being an auctioneer's helper,
then?"

"No, I don't. I might like you, but Gissem and
Fillow treat me awful."

"In what way?"

"Well, in the first place they don't half feed
me, and then they don't pay me the wages they
promised."

"What did they promise you?"

"Five dollars a week to start on, and ten dollars
when I was worth it. I've been with them a long
time, but I was never able to get a cent out of
them."

"Supposing you had the money, would you go
home?" asked Matt kindly, for he saw that the
boy's better feelings had been touched.

"I don't know if I would dare. Ma might whip

me and have me sent to the reform school, or something like that."

"I don't think she would—not if you promise to
turn over a new leaf. I should think you would
rather go home than remain where you have to
work for nothing."

"I guess I would go home if I had a railroad
ticket and some clothes fit to wear. You can see
how this suit looks," and Tom Inwold showed up
his ragged elbows and patched trousers.

"I'll see if I can do something for you," said
Matt.

When Andy came back he told his partner Tom
Inwold's story. To this the boy himself added the
tale of his hardships while with the rival auctioneers, and added that he was very sorry he had
endeavored to do any injury to the stock in the
store.

"I believe he means it," said Matt, as he and
Andy walked a little to one side. "And I would
like to do something for the lad, for his mother's
sake as much as his own."

"I think I can fix it," replied Andy. "I'll have
a talk with this Gissem."

"He ought to pay the boy something for his
work."

" I reckon he will—when I tell him that he is liable to arrest for enticing the boy from home."

Andy told Tom Inwold to accompany him to the store next door. At first the boy hung back, but when Andy promised that he would take the responsibility of the coming interview entirely upon his own shoulders, the lad consented to go along.

They were gone nearly an hour, and during that time Matt heard some pretty loud talking through the partition which separated the two stores. But when Andy and Tom Inwold came back he saw by their faces that they had triumphed.

"At first Gissem was in for facing me down," said Andy. "Said he had nothing to do with the boy, and all that. But I threatened him with immediate arrest, and promised to have the mother of the boy here to testify against him, and then he weakened, and at length gave Tom thirty dollars, with which to buy a new suit of clothes, a pair of shoes, a hat, and a railroad ticket, upon conditions that he would not be prosecuted. I reckon he was badly scared, too."

Matt was much pleased. Leaving Andy in charge of the store, he went out to dinner, taking Tom Inwold along with him. After the meal the wearing apparel was purchased and donned, and then they made their way to the depot. Here a ticket for

Plainfield was procured, and the young auctioneer saw to it that the boy boarded the proper train.

"I'll never forget you, never," said Tom Inwold on parting, and he never has, nor has Mrs. Inwold, who was grateful to the last degree for what Matt had been instrumental in doing for her.

On the following morning, on going down to the store to open up, Andy and Matt saw that the entire stock of the store adjoining had been removed during the night. Gissem had been fearful of trouble, despite what Andy had promised, and had taken time by the forelock, and left for parts unknown. The young auctioneers never met him or his partner again.

By having the entire field to themselves the young auctioneers did a splendid business, and when they were ready to pack up and start for Scranton they found that they had cleared nearly ninety dollars by their stay in Wilkes-Barre.

In the meantime the weather had been growing steadily colder, and they found it necessary to invest in a second-hand robe to keep them warm when driving.

"It looks a bit like snow," remarked Andy, as they drove out of the city one morning. "I hope we don't catch it before we reach where we are going to. A snowstorm in the mountains is not a very pleasant thing to encounter."

"We must run our chances," returned Matt, and Billy was urged forward, and soon the city outskirts were left far behind.

The sun had shone for awhile, but about nine o'clock it went under a heavy cloud. Then it began to get slightly warmer, and Andy was certain that snow was coming.

His prediction was fulfilled. By ten o'clock it was snowing furiously, and by eleven the ground was covered to the depth of half a foot.

"That settles it; we can't make Scranton to-day, nor even Pittston," said Matt. "We had better hunt up some sort of a house with a barn attached, where we can put up."

But Andy was for continuing the journey, so onward they went, until at last, just before the noon hour, they found the road getting too heavy for Billy. They went down into a hollow which the falling snow had covered, and there the wagon remained, despite every effort to budge it.

They looked around in some dismay. Not even a house nor a building of any sort was in sight.

"This is a pretty pickle," muttered Andy. "I wish we had followed your advice and sought shelter."

"We've got to do something," returned Matt. " If we stay here we'll be completely snowed under. The snow is coming down thicker every minute. What's to be done?"

Ah! what was to be done? That was a question not easy to answer. Both of the young auctioneers were much disturbed.

CHAPTER XXXVI.

LOST IN THE SNOW.

It was not a pleasant outlook, stuck in a deep hollow on the road with the snow coming down furiously. Already the ground was covered to the depth of a foot or more, and around the heavily-laden wagon a drift was forming which soon reached above the axles.

"We must do something, that's certain," muttered Matt, as he sprang to Billy's head for at least the fifth time. "Come, old fellow, can't you stir it up a bit?"

Andy ran to the back of the wagon and placed his shoulder against the case there strapped on. But though the two and Billy, the horse, did their best, the auction wagon remained where it was.

"It's no use," groaned Andy, as he stopped to catch his breath. "We are stuck as hard as if we were planted here, and it looks as if we would have to remain here for some time."

"We must move on," returned Matt desperately.

"In a few hours night will be coming on, and we'll be completely covered."

"The snow is coming down faster than ever, and the wind is rising. Maybe we are going to have a blizzard. If we do, Heaven help us!"

"Let us take those cases of goods off," suggested the young auctioneer after a moment of thought. "That will lighten the load for Billy somewhat."

The big packing boxes were unstrapped and let down in the snow. They were followed by every other article which could be removed from the turn-out without damage.

Then Billy was once more urged to go on, Matt and Andy pushing with all their strength in the meanwhile. The wheels of the wagon and the axles creaked and then moved forward slowly.

"Hurrah! we've got it started!" shouted Matt joyfully. "Get up, Billy! get up!"

And the horse really did strain every muscle until, two minutes later, the wagon was out of the hollow and up on the ridge of a little hill.

"Thank fortune we are out of that!" exclaimed Andy. "Now what is to be done?"

"We had better strap the cases in place again and continue on our way."

"The cases are awfully heavy. I wonder if we can't hide them somewhere and come back for them later! The snow is not melting, so that won't hurt them."

The matter was talked over, and finally they decided to leave the two cases, which had not been opened, and were well packed, under a big tree near the roadside. The cases were removed to the spot without delay, placed upon a couple of dead trees and covered with brush.

Then they moved on again, Andy leading the horse, and Matt going on ahead to inspect the road, and thus avoid getting into another hollow.

It was bitterly cold, and having nothing but a light overcoat on, the young auctioneer was chilled to the bone. He was compelled to caper about and clap his hands continually to keep from being frozen. The snow, now fine and hard, beat into his face mercilessly, and to protect himself from this he pulled his hat far down over his eyes, and tied his handkerchief over his mouth and nose.

But the hardships of the storm were not to be endured for long. A quarter of a mile further on they came to a large farmhouse, situated some little distance back from the road. In the rear was a barn and a cow-shed.

Running ahead, Matt knocked upon the door of the house. It was opened by an elderly farmer, who was smoking, and who held a paper in his hand.

"Good-afternoon," said the young auctioneer. "Can we get shelter here for ourselves and our horse? We are willing to pay for the accommodation."

"What's the matter? Caught on the road?" returned the farmer pleasantly.

"Yes, sir," and Matt briefly narrated the particulars.

"Drive right around to the barn," were the farmer's welcome words. "I'll open up for you and make your horse comfortable enough."

And reaching for his hat and coat, he put them on and came outside.

Andy was not slow to drive Billy into shelter. The barn was a large one, and far from filled, and the wagon went in without difficulty.

As soon as the horse had been cared for, the young auctioneers followed the farmer back to the house. The family had just finished their dinner, but set to work at once to prepare food for the half-frozen and exhausted travelers.

While Matt and Andy were warming up they told the farmer about the cases which had been left on the road.

"I suppose they ought not to be left there too

long," said Andy. " If I had a light wagon and a pair of strong horses I would go after them as soon as I've had something to eat."

" Don't you mind ; I'll go after 'em for you," said the farmer. " I've got Sam and Bess, and they can pull through most anything. Perhaps after you've had dinner it will be too late."

" Well, if you get them we will pay you whatever it is worth," returned Matt's partner.

The farmer set about the trip without delay, and just as Andy and Matt were called to the dining-table he drove out of the yard.

The meal was a good one, there being plenty to eat and all of it well served. To the two half-famished ones it seemed to be about the best meal they had ever tasted.

After it was over they sat down by the fire and began to chat with the farmer's wife, a motherly creature of the same age as her husband. Every five minutes Matt would walk to the window to see if the farmer was yet returning.

It was nearly an hour before Mr. Pearsall, for such was the farmer's name, drove up to the door. Matt and Andy ran out to meet him, and were relieved to learn that the cases of goods had been brought in good condition. They were taken around to the barn and there transferred to their original places on the auction wagon.

Mr. Pearsall was curious to know something of their business, and when they were once more in the house the two young auctioneers told their story, to which both the farmer and his wife listened with deep interest.

As it continued to snow, Matt and Andy decided to remain at the farmhouse over night, and arrangements were made to that effect. They spent a pleasant evening, and all hands retired early.

In the morning, much to their joy, they found that the snow had stopped coming down, and that the sun was shining brightly. They had an early breakfast, and then, after settling with Mr. Pearsall, who did not wish cash, but took goods his wife desired instead, they set off for Pittston, which was scarcely half a mile distant.

Billy had had a good rest, and the city mentioned above was reached in a short while. Here they arranged for an extra horse, that was hitched up in front of their own. In this manner they started for Scranton with more confidence.

The road was as rocky and uneven as before, but it being bright and clear, they were enabled to avoid hollows with ease. They stopped at Taylor for dinner, and arrived in Scranton an hour before nightfall, tired out, but happy to think that their journey, for the balance of the week at least, was over.

As soon as they had settled in a vacant store Matt left Andy in charge and hurried to the post-office, to look for a letter from Ida Bartlett. He was not disappointed; the letter was there, and he read it with deep interest.

" Since receiving your letter," she wrote, " I have been watching Mr. Fenton closely, and I am satisfied that he is much disturbed over the fact that Mr. Gaston has left his employ and that he was threatened with exposure. I have also taken the liberty to write to Mr. Gaston, but have, as yet, received no reply. Will write again as soon as he answers. It is a pity you cannot find out what became of your poor father and the papers."

CHAPTER XXXVII.

MORE OF AUCTION LIFE.

"Yes, I would give every cent I am worth, and more, to learn what did become of father," said Matt to Andy, after he had allowed his partner to peruse the letter.

"I have no doubt you would, Matt," returned Andy feelingly. "I can imagine how much it worries you—not knowing if he is dead or alive. But you must keep a stout heart and trust to the future to clear up the mystery."

"I'm trying to do that, but, Andy, it's hard work," and Matt's handsome face took on an unusually sober look.

Knowing that nothing could be gained by discussing the matter, which had been talked over a score of times previously, Andy changed the subject. Business had opened very well, and he wished to go out and have some circulars printed, by which even a larger crowd might be attracted to the sale.

It remained clear for two days, and during that

time both of the young auctioneers were kept busy from eight o'clock in the morning until eleven at night.

On the third day it began to grow warmer, and by noon it was raining steadily.

" Well, never mind, the rain will wash the snow away, and if it only stays clear afterward we will have a chance to get on to Carbondale," was Andy's cheerful comment.

Seeing that Matt could get along very well alone, he left the store in the afternoon to buy a heavy overcoat at some clothing establishment. If he procured what he wished, Matt was to buy one also.

Left to himself, the young auctioneer did what he could to attract trade, but without success. He waited on the few customers who had drifted in, but when they were gone found himself alone.

Rather than have the time hang heavily upon his hands he began to clean up the stock. Cutlery and spoons need constant care to keep them looking bright, and Matt was, therefore, never at a loss for employment.

While he was hard at work shining up some silver-plated ware which was slightly tarnished through handling, the door of the store was flung open violently, and a large, heavily-built man stag-

gered in. At a glance Matt saw that the man was
much the worse for the liquor he had drunk.

"Say, is this an auction store?" grunted the man,
as he tried to walk up to the counter with some
show of steadiness.

"It is," returned the young auctioneer briefly.
Of all persons to deal with he hated a drunken man
the worst.

"It is, hey—a genuine auction store?" went on
the tipsy individual.

"Yes. What can I do for you?" and Matt put
the silverware he was handling away.

"I want to buy a pistol."

Matt was surprised at this statement, and he was
was also alarmed. The tipsy man was certainly not
the person to have a firearm in his possession.

"You wish a pistol?" he said slowly.

"That's me, boy! Hand out the best pistol you
have in the place! I don't want any toy pop-gun
remember!"

And the man glared at Matt as though the boy
were his one personal enemy.

"Excuse me, but I hardly think I have a pistol to
suit you," replied the young auctioneer, thinking it
best to discourage the man if possible. "You had
better go to a regular firearms store."

"I ain't a-going nowhere but here!" growled the

would-be customer, as he gave a lurch against the counter. "I want a pistol; best you got, understand?"

"I understand, but I haven't any pistol for you," Matt replied steadily. He wished Andy would come back.

"What! do you mean to say you refuse to sell me a pistol?" howled the man savagely. "Let me tell you, boy, that I have ample means for reimbursing you."

"I haven't any pistol for you, sir. You had better go elsewhere."

"Won't go, understand, I won't go! Let me see them pistols in that show-case, and be quick about it!"

Matt was now growing alarmed. The man was just intoxicated enough to be thoroughly ugly, and might try to do him harm should he refuse the request which had been made. Yet he realized more than ever that the man was not the one to be trusted with a firearm.

"I do not care to show you the pistols," was all the young auctioneer could say. "You must go elsewhere if you wish one."

"Won't sell me one, hey?"

"No, I will not."

"Why?"

"I have my reasons."

"You're awfully smart, boy; most too smart to live! But I am going to have what I want, understand that!"

With unsteady steps the man walked to the rear end of the counter and came around to the inner side. He was met by Matt, who, becoming alarmed, had picked up the butt-end of a fishing-rod with which to defend himself.

"You can't come back here, sir."

"Oh, yes, I can."

"I say you cannot. The best thing you can do is to go elsewhere."

"What! do you threaten me?"

"I want you to understand that you cannot come back here. I told you I did not wish to sell you a pistol, and that ought to be enough."

"Want to fight, boy?" demanded the man, scowling savagely and doubling up his fists.

"No, I do not wish to fight. I merely wish to be left alone."

Matt had hardly spoken when the tipsy man hurled himself forward, intending to catch the young auctioneer by the throat. But Matt was too quick for him. He stepped backward, and the consequence was that the man went headlong, striking the floor with such force that every article in the store shook and rattled.

"You—you young villain!" panted the tipsy man, as he attempted to rise to his feet. "What do you mean by such conduct? Help me up, do you hear?"

"I hear, but I am not going to assist you until you promise to leave at once," returned Matt.

"I'm going to look at those pistols first," growled the intoxicated one, and by holding fast to the counter he managed, but not without much difficulty, to rise to his feet once more. "That's a fine way to treat a gentleman!"

"It was your own fault. You had no business to try to catch me by the throat."

"And you had no business to be saucy, understand, boy, saucy? I never allow any one to be saucy to me. Now them pistols, and no more nonsense."

Instead of replying, Matt tried to push the man out from behind the counter. The young auctioneer thought that if he could get him out near the door he would then be able to summon assistance and have the tipsy individual taken away.

Evidently the man suspected his intention. He declined to be pushed back, and seeing what he considered a good chance, he hurled himself at

Matt once more, and this time both rolled to the floor.

In going down, the young auctioneer struck his head upon the sharp corner of a box. He was partly stunned, and for several seconds could not make a movement in his own favor. The piece of the fishing-rod flew out of his hand, and this his opponent picked up.

" I'll teach you to talk to a gentleman like myself !" growled the tipsy man, and he aimed a blow at the young auctioneer's head with the weapon he had secured.

The blow failed to reach its mark, but undismayed by his failure to injure Matt, the man gathered himself together and prepared for a second attack.

CHAPTER XXXVIII.

A SURPRISING DISCOVERY.

IT looked as if the young auctioneer was in for a serious time of it. As has been said, the would-be purchaser of a pistol was just drunk enough to be ugly and unreasonable. He had refused to leave the auction store, and now he was bent upon doing mischief to the boy who had failed to treat him as he fancied he ought to be served.

" Now, how do you like that, you young rascal ?" growled the man, as he brought the end of the fishing-rod down for a second time.

" I don't like it at all," returned Matt, as he recovered sufficiently to dodge out of the way, although the stick came uncomfortably close to his ears. " Let me up at once."

" Not much, boy, not much ! I'm going to teach you a lesson to be civil to customers !"

" You are getting yourself into serious trouble."

" Ho! ho! I reckon I am able to take care of myself."

Once again the man sought to strike Matt, and this time he succeeded. The blow landed upon the young auctioneer's shoulder, and caused him to cry out with pain.

At that instant the door opened, and Andy entered the store, carrying on his arm the new overcoat he had just purchased.

"What's the matter, Matt?" he cried, in quick alarm.

"Help me, Andy! This drunken man is trying to knock me out with that stick!"

The senior partner of the firm needed no second call for assistance. Without hesitation he flung the overcoat on a packing case, and rushing up to Matt's assailant, caught him by the collar and dragged him from behind the counter.

"Let me—me go!" spluttered the tipsy individual. "Let go my collar!"

"Don't you do it, Andy!" and Matt sprang to his feet as quickly as he could.

"I don't intend to," was Andy's determined answer. "What's the meaning of this trouble?"

"He wouldn't let me look at the pistols," whined the tipsy man, collapsing now that he saw he was powerless to do any more injury.

"I didn't think he was in fit condition to look at anything," put in Matt.

"You had no right to abuse my partner," said Andy, sure that Matt was in the right of the altercation. "Now you get right out of here, and don't show your face again."

And Andy shoved the man toward the door, which he had left partly open.

The tipsy man began to remonstrate, and wanted to fight both of them. He grew quite abusive, and threatened to wreck all the things in the establishment. Before he could carry out his threat, however, Andy and Matt landed him out on his back on the sidewalk and beckoned to a passing policeman.

"What! so it's you again!" cried the officer, on seeing the intoxicated individual. "I thought you had warning enough at the hotel. What has he been doing?" he asked of Matt.

"He got mad because I wouldn't let him handle the pistols in the place."

"The pistols?"

"Yes, sir. He insisted upon seeing the best pistol we had, and I wouldn't accommodate him. I thought it might be dangerous. Of course he would want cartridges, and then he might go off and shoot somebody."

"That was his intention. He got into a row in the hotel on the next block, and the clerk says he threatened to shoot the proprietor. I suppose he was bent on getting the pistol to do it with. Just you come with me, and I'll give you a chance to sober up."

The tipsy man remonstrated, and tried to make the policeman believe that the rows at the hotel and at the store were only jokes. But the officer would not listen, and took the drunken individual to the station-house, where, later on, he was sentenced to thirty days in the county jail for disturbing the peace.

"That's another side of the auction business," said Matt, after he and Andy were left alone. "And I must confess it's a side I don't like. It was lucky you came along when you did."

"An intoxicated man never makes a good customer, Matt. Some store-keepers try to get his money away from him, but, as for me, I want nothing to do with him."

The blow on the shoulder had not injured Matt, and soon the incident, exciting as it had been, was almost forgotten. Andy had struck a bargain, as he termed it, in the purchase of his new overcoat, and he wished Matt to go off at once and get one like it.

"They are selling about two dozen off at bottom price," he said. "And you want to lose no time if you wish to get fitted. It is the first store on the third block above here."

"All right, I'll go, Andy, for I can't do without the overcoat," and off Matt started, never once dreaming of what was going to happen on that simple little shopping trip.

Matt located the clothing shop without difficulty. It was quite well filled with customers, but he soon found the salesman who had served Andy, and this young man did not keep him waiting any longer than was absolutely necessary.

There were three overcoats which just fitted Matt, and he hesitated as to which to take. He tried them all on, but could not decide the question.

"I'll take them to the daylight and examine them," he said, and walked from the center of the store, which was lighted by gas, toward the show window.

Here he began to examine each overcoat critically. One was black, the other brown, and third a dark blue. Matt rather fancied the dark blue.

While he was handling over the dark-blue coat, the form of a ragged man darkened the side of the show window furthest from the door. With hardly a thought, Matt looked up to see who it was.

Then the heart of the young auctioneer seemed

to fairly stop beating. The ragged man on the pavement outside was *his father!*

With a sharp cry that startled every one in the establishment, Matt dashed down the garments he held and made a rush for the door. At the same moment the man outside, catching one glimpse of Matt's face, put up both his hands ·to his forehead and sped up the street as if running for his life!

" What's the matter with that young fellow ?"

" What's the matter with the man ?"

" Say, come back here !"

" Did he steal anything ?"

These and a score of other cries rang out in quick succession. But Matt paid no attention, nor did he stop to offer any explanation to the astonished clothing salesman. He had seen his father, his father for whom he had been searching so long and so earnestly! He could tell that face, as haggard and white as it was, among a million.

Away sped the man up the street, and on after him came Matt, running as he had never run before. He could not understand why his parent should thus try to get away from him. But he did not stop to reason on the matter. He wanted to reach his father, that was all, and he strained every muscle to accomplish his effort.

But although Matt was a good runner, the man

he was after appeared well able to keep beyond his reach. Evidently some dreadful fear urged him on, for many times he would look back over his shoulder, and each time pass his hands over his forehead, as if to wipe the sight from his brain and memory.

Soon several blocks had been passed, and then the man turned a corner, and started toward the poorer section of the city. Matt continued to follow for half a dozen blocks further. Then he saw his father dart into the open hallway of a half-tumbled-down tenement.

When he reached the building the young auctioneer peered into the hallway, but could see no one. Several little girls were playing upon the sidewalk, and he asked them if they had seen any one go in.

"Crazy Will just went in," replied one of the girls. "Guess he has gone up to his room in the garret."

"Crazy Will!" murmured Matt to himself. "Poor father! How thankful I am that I have found you at last!"

And trembling with emotion, he hurried up the rickety stairs until he reached the door of the apartment which one of the girls pointed out as that occupied by Crazy Will.

CHAPTER XXXIX.

A MYSTERY CLEARED UP.

THE door of the garret room was closed, and when Matt tried the knob, he found that it was also locked. He knocked lightly upon it.

At first there was no response. Then a weak voice, which he could but faintly recognize as that of his father, asked sharply:

"Who's there? What do you want? Why don't you go away and leave me alone?"

"Father! father! come and open the door!" exclaimed Matt, his voice trembling as it had never trembled before.

"Who speaks? Go away, I say, and leave a poor old man alone!"

"Father, it is me, Matt! Don't you remember me?"

"Matt! Matt! Oh, no, Matt was lost when his mother was lost and the money! Yes, the money, mother, and Matt! Too bad! Go away, and don't persecute me!"

"No, father, you are mistaken. I am here, father—your only son, Matt. Please open the door."

"You are fooling me! Didn't you fool me about Matt only last week and throw a pail of water on me, and call me Crazy Will? Go away, I say!"

"No, father, I will not go away! You must open the door! You *must!* I have been hunting for you so long—ever since mother died and you disappeared, and now that I have found you, we shall never separate again. Open the door; do, please."

These words, spoken with an intensity which cannot be described, had the necessary effect upon the poor, weak-minded man inside of the garret room. Matt heard him move slowly toward the door, and then heard the key turn in the lock. The next instant the door opened, and the boy sprang into the room and caught his father around the neck.

"Oh, father, don't you know me?" he cried, with deep emotion. "It is Matt, your only son!"

He looked his father steadily in the eyes, the tears meanwhile coursing freely down his cheeks. Mr. Lincoln returned the gaze for a moment, then the wild look died out of his eyes, and his breast heaved and he gave a deep sob.

"Matt! Matt! It is really you! My son! my son!"

He caught the boy in his arms and hugged him to his breast, sobbing the meanwhile like a little child. He spoke of his wife and her death, of his lost money, and a hundred other things, and then, in the midst of it all, threw up his arms and sank to the floor in a dead faint.

A less courageous boy than Matt would have been badly scared. But he knew of these fainting spells, for his father had had them years before and had always come out of them feeling weaker in body, it was true, but always clearer in mind.

In one corner of the room lay an old mattress, and upon this he placed his father's form. Then he opened the tightly-closed window and began to bathe his father's forehead with some water that stood in a cracked pitcher near by.

Two of the girls that had told him about Crazy Will had followed him up the tenement stairs and were now standing outside of the garret-room door, staring at all that was going on. Matt called them in.

"Do either of you want to earn twenty-five cents?" he asked.

"What doin'?" asked the older of the two girls promptly:

"I want you to deliver a message for me."

"Where to?"

Matt mentioned the auction store and described its location. The girl said she knew where it was and would willingly take a message there.

"Don't yer want a doctor?" she asked.

"Not yet. You take this note and it will be all right. But you must not lose a minute."

"I'll run all the way," replied the girl.

Taking out a notebook he carried, Matt hastily scribbled down the following brief message:

"ANDY: I have found my father. Come with the bearer at once.   MATT."

This he folded up and addressed to his partner. In another minute the girl was flying down the tenement stairs, two steps at a time, the other girl close behind her.

When they were gone Matt closed the door and again turned his attention to his father.

Mr. Lincoln's eyes were still closed, but by putting his ear down to his parent's chest, Matt found that his father was breathing quite regularly. He continued to bathe his parent's forehead and also fanned him with a newspaper which was lying by.

While waiting for his father to come to again, Matt could not help but gaze at the surroundings. The garret room was small and bare of furniture, containing nothing but the mattress, a broken-down stove, and a few cracked dishes. There was half a loaf of stale bread beside the dishes, and nothing else to eat was in sight.

" What a place to live in!" murmured the boy to himself. " Poor father! Poor father!"

He again bent over the motionless form, and it was not long before he had the satisfaction of seeing his father open his eyes.

" Matt, is it really you, or is this another one of those tantalizing dreams?" asked Mr. Lincoln feebly, as he essayed to rise to a sitting position.

" It is really I, father," returned the son gently. " You had better lie still for awhile. Your run exhausted you."

" How thankful I am that it is really you! But there must be some mistake. I have dreamed of these things before. That is why I ran away."

" There is no mistake now, father, it is really and truly I," and Matt bent lower and wound his arms around his father's neck. " You have nothing more to fear, father. Just rely on me for everything."

" I will, Matt, I will! I know it is you, now that you are so close to me!"

" And, father, you must promise that you will not run away again."

" I promise, Matt. My mind was upset—it's up-

set yet, I'm afraid. But I won't leave you, Matt:
I won't leave you. I used to imagine I saw you,
and then the boys on the street would plague me
and call me Crazy Will. But that's all over now,
thank Heaven! That's all over now!"

CHAPTER XL.

THE MINING SHARES—CONCLUSION.

IN less than half an hour Andy reached the garret room, and Matt told his partner his story. Andy was introduced to Mr. Lincoln as a friend who could be trusted in all things, and although the weak-minded man was suspicious of all strangers, he made no demonstration against his son's companion.

" I wish to take him to some quiet place, where he can have the best of medical attention," said Matt to Andy. " Do you think you can find such a place ? I do not dare to leave him yet."

" I will do my best," returned Andy.

He went off in search of the right place, and in an hour came back, accompanied by a pleasant man fifty or sixty years of age, whom he introduced as Dr. Zabrinsky.

" The doctor will take your father into his own home," he said. " He has two patients suffering from mental troubles and makes a specialty of such things. He will do his best."

Matt was pleased by the medical man's appearance, and after some little conversation, a carriage was called, and Mr. Lincoln was removed, accompanied by Matt, to the doctor's private sanitarium. Andy was left behind to go over Mr. Lincoln's meager effects and bring away anything of value.

At the doctor's home the almost helpless man was made as comfortable as possible. He was inclined to become excited over what had happened, but the doctor administered an opiate, and he soon after sank into a gentle slumber.

When Andy reached the house some time later his face betoken that he had something of unusual interest to tell. He bore a package of papers in his hand, and these he handed over to Matt.

"I found then stuck in the mattress," he said. "They are papers in reference to the mining shares your father purchased from Randolph Fenton. From what you have told me, I believe Fenton swindled your father. As soon as your father is well enough to be left I would send for that Mr. Gaston and have the matter looked up."

Matt examined the papers with keen interest. He became satisfied that Andy was right, and determined to act upon his suggestions.

Dr. Zabrinsky was true to his word. He did all that was possible for the sufferer, and between his medical skill and Matt's watchful care, Mr. Lincoln recovered rapidly. Once in a great while his mind would take on a flighty turn, but Matt was watchful and always calmed him down, and at the end of six months the man whose mind had been so strangely affected was as rational and well as ever.

Long before this time Matt made a trip to New York and called upon Ida Bartlett at her new place of business. They had a long conversation concerning Randolph Fenton and his methods of selling stocks and shares.

At the end of this talk Matt made inquiries concerning Mr. Gaston's whereabouts. He learned that the former clerk was in Bridgeport, Connecticut, and telegraphed that he wished to see him without delay. On the following Friday morning Mr. Gaston presented himself at the hotel at which Matt was stopping.

The young auctioneer went over his entire story and produced the papers which had been in his father's possession. He promised Gaston a liberal reward should they succeed in forcing Randolph Fenton to make proper restitution for a transaction that was undoubtedly criminal upon its face.

The old book-keeper at once consented to do what he could. He called in a lawyer of thorough experience, and several affidavits were made out, and a search made for Mr. Lincoln's rightful shares, for the ones Randolph Fenton had assigned to him had been some of a similar name but of far less value. Then all hands marched down to the broker's office.

Randolph Fenton was somewhat surprised to see Matt, and he turned slightly pale when Gaston confronted him, accompanied by the lawyer and another man he knew was a private detective.

Without preliminaries, the lawyer explained the object of the visit. As he proceeded the broker grew paler and paler, and he clutched the arms of his chair nervously.

"You—you are mistaken!" he finally gasped out. "That transaction was perfectly legitimate. This is a plot on the part of that man and that boy to ruin my reputation!"

"It is no plot, Mr. Fenton," put in Matt. "For my poor father's sake as well as my own, I ask for justice; that is all. Your actions unbalanced my father's mind, and if I wanted to be hard-hearted I would not rest until you were behind the prison bars."

"Stuff and nonsense! This is all a put-up job——"

"Don't get excited, Mr. Fenton," said the lawyer pointedly. "The boy is letting you down very easily, to my way of thinking."

"Tut-tut! I won't listen to a word! I want you all to leave this office and stop this farce!"

"If we have to leave without satisfaction you will go with Mr. Briarly, the detective," cried Matt. "Now you can take your choice. I am no longer your office boy, and you cannot twist me around your finger."

These words filled Randolph Fenton with rage. He wanted to abuse everybody within hearing, but both the lawyer and the detective cut him short by threatening him with immediate arrest. Finally he asked for time in which to consider the case.

This was granted, but after they left Matt instructed the detective to keep a close watch on the man, fearful that Fenton, who, according to Mr. Gaston's statement, was in bad favor in a number of places, would convert what securities he held into cash and leave for parts unknown.

It was well that Matt did this, for on the following night the detective captured the broker just as the latter was boarding a train at the Grand Central depot. He had a satchel full of money with him, and in his card case was found a railroad ticket for Montreal, Canada. Randolph Fenton was placed under arrest, and then all of his many misdeeds were thoroughly investigated and exposed.

Out of the wreckage the swindling broker had

left behind him Matt was able to secure three-
fourths of the rightful shares of mining stock for
his father. These shares had gone up in value and
were found to be worth close on to fifty-eight thousand dollars. To Matt, who, in his wanderings
around, had learned the true value of money, it
seemed a fortune.

"You won't want any more of the auction business," said Andy. "You will have your hands full
taking care of that money and your father."

"Yes, I guess my days as a young auctioneer are
over," returned Matt. "I want to get a better edu-
cation if possible, and thus fit myself for something
higher in life."

"What about your share in the business? I can't
buy it out just yet."

"I have talked it over with father, Andy, and I
have decided to make you a present of it. You deserve it, for ever since we met you have been a real
brother to me. Make what you can out of the business, and if you ever get in a tight corner don't
hesitate to come to me, and I will do what I can for
you."

Andy demurred at Matt's generosity, but was
finally persuaded to accept the gift. He settled in
Middletown for the winter and did very well. In
the spring he started on his travels again, and by

fall had made enough to open a good-sized picture and art store in New York City on Fourteenth street. He still runs the store and is making money fast, much to the disgust of Caleb Gulligan, who grows poorer each year.

After Matt left the auction business he settled down with his father in a quiet home on the Hudson River, not many miles above the great metropolis. He took care of his father until the next autumn, when Mr. Lincoln felt sufficiently recovered to go into business, and purchased the controlling interest in a large flour and feed establishment. The business is very prosperous. Ida Bartlett is stenographer and confidential clerk to the firm, and has a well-paying position, which will remain open for her so long as the kind-hearted young woman cares to occupy it. Matt did not fail to keep his former determination to give her a handsome Christmas present, and the two are likely to be life-long friends.

As for Matt himself, he has just finished a course at Columbia College, and next month will become the junior partner in a promising young law firm. Let us wish him every success, for the honest and fearless lad who was once the Young Auctioneer deserves it.

THE END.

www.ingramcontent.com/pod-product-compliance
Lightning Source LLC
Chambersburg PA
CBHW060533030726
47498CB00004B/1178